HONOR IN THE MOUNTAIN REFUGE

CALL OF THE ROCKIES ~ BOOK 6

MISTY M. BELLER

Misty M. Beller
BOOKS

ISBN-13 Trade Paperback: 978-1-954810-05-1

ISBN-13 Large Print Paperback: 978-1-954810-14-3

ISBN-13 Casebound Hardback: 978-1-954810-15-0

And I will bring the blind by a way that they knew not;
I will lead them in paths that they have not known:
I will make darkness light before them, and crooked things straight.
These things will I do unto them, and not forsake them.

Isaiah 42:16 (KJV)

CHAPTER 1

Summer, 1831
Clearwater River Valley, Future Idaho Territory

*T*he fine hairs along Telípe's neck stood on end, and she turned to scan the woods around her—not an easy feat with the babe weighing down her belly.

Was there an animal watching her? Or could there be a person scouting out there, unseen?

She peered through the summer leaves covering the trees, but all appeared still. Maybe the sensation had only come from sweat trickling down her neck.

Turning back to the fruit bushes, she pushed aside the branches and reached for a cluster of chokecherries. At least the trees offered shade and a bit of a breeze, unlike the hot, smoky lodge she'd escaped. With all her family lounging or milling about the place—including Pisákas, the man her brother seemed to constantly be placing in her path, and his young motherless son—she could barely breathe, much less think.

Of course, she couldn't breathe well anyway, as the baby filled every empty space inside her. She slipped a hand under

1

her belly to better support the mass at her middle, then reached for another cluster of cherries.

She'd never expected her final days before confinement to look like this. The home she'd thought would be hers to tend for the rest of her life, gone. Just when she'd finally found a measure of fulfillment caring for her new husband, he'd been taken away too.

Now, she'd returned to the lodge of her family. Actually, her eldest brother's home now, for when their parents died, he'd taken over as the principle man of the family. Thankfully, he'd married, bringing his new wife and her grandmother to live with them. Both women were kind and generous. Ámtiz willingly took over care for Telípe and Síkem's two younger brothers, and the young woman's patience with the boys never ended. They'd all taken to calling the older woman simply *the grandmother*, and the entire group had found a comfortable rhythm.

One that Telípe wasn't quite part of. Since she'd returned, she seemed to be more in the way than anything. No wonder Síkem wanted to marry her off to his friend.

She used the back of her wrist to swipe the sweat trickling into her eyes, then waved off a mosquito and reached for another cluster of cherries. After pushing a branch aside, she studied what remained of the fruit. All green. Better to wait for them to ripen.

Turning to slip out of the thick brush, her sleeve caught on a limb. She elbowed the branch aside, then waddled forward, grabbing a tree to help her up the hill.

Every move took more effort with the babe so large in her belly. She couldn't possibly get any bigger in the final few days. There was no room. Once she pulled herself out of the hollow, she paused to catch her breath, leaning against a trunk for support.

Her gaze wandered through the woods around her. In the

past, the leafy growth had been a sign of new life. But she couldn't summon the strength to feel hopeful now.

A movement snagged her focus, and she narrowed her attention to that spot. Perhaps only a squirrel, but all kinds of animals roamed these trees. Big predatory creatures.

And predatory men.

The movement stilled, but something didn't appear right among the limbs overhead. Thick leaves covered much of the area, but something showed between the green.

Leather? Was that the brown of buckskins? She gripped a tree as she strained to make out what she was seeing.

Then another movement flashed. A face appeared between leaves. Not a bear or a wildcat. A man.

Her heart thundered in her chest. *Not a man. Not again.*

She turned to flee, though the futility of the act swept through her as she faced thick tree growth that would only slow her down. In her condition, she could barely toddle, much less run. She was more likely to fall down the wooded hill than to outrun an able-bodied man.

But she couldn't let herself be caught again. She may not fare so well this time.

Grabbing her belly to support its weight, she reached for a tree to push off from. Yet she'd barely taken two steps before a voice sounded from behind.

"*Tayógosa.*" *Wait.*

He'd spoken the word in her tongue. Did that mean he *wasn't* part of another Blackfoot war party come to take captives as slaves for their people? Maybe he was only one of the braves from a neighboring town out hunting.

But she still felt the urge to flee. She paused and made herself turn to face him.

He'd come down from the tree and now stood beside the trunk. Definitely a full-grown man, taller than most with broad shoulders. A flash of memory slipped through her. She knew another brave with wide shoulders like that.

But she didn't allow her mind to form his shape or his handsome features.

Instead, she honed her gaze on this man's face. A jolt coursed through her. *It couldn't be.* Was this a vision? Surely...

He took a step nearer, moving into a patch of sunlight. A gasp slipped out even as her heart raced into her throat.

Hope and panic warred through her, and she stepped back, though her feet were too frozen to the ground to turn and run. Had he returned to recapture her? Maybe he'd realized he shouldn't have been so kind the last time, shouldn't have protected her from the other warriors when his band had kidnapped her before.

Had they sent him on a quest to retake the captive himself in order to keep his place among them?

Fear overtook every other emotion, and she spun away from him. Grasping for first one trunk, then the next, she scrambled through the trees. Down the hill.

"Amkakáiz."

The word he barked only slowed her down a tiny bit. Surely he wasn't saying that he came in peace. Did he even know what that idea meant? His people prided themselves on how many captives they took of her tribe. And how did he know so much of her Nimiipuu tongue? He'd spoken only a couple words the last time she'd seen him.

She kept running, sliding down the slope, nearly seated and gripping the trees to keep from tumbling.

"Telípe!"

Her name on his lips slowed her more than anything else. Something in his tone reminded her of his kindness before. He'd been so careful with her, especially after he learned of the baby, always making sure she had enough food and furs to keep warm through the snows.

She finally let herself stop, struggling to take in breaths. The need to run away fought against her exhausted limbs. She craned to look back at him, though her bulky body couldn't turn with the awkward position she was in.

Chogan took another step forward, his hand outstretched as though to calm a flighty horse. "Amkakáiz." This time he accompanied the word with the sign for peace. Did he really mean it?

She stared at his face for signs of his true intentions. Though he looked every bit the strong warrior he had before, his eyes held kindness. And also something more, a shadow they hadn't possessed before. Maybe the distance between them caused the expression.

He motioned for her to stand. "I will not hurt you."

She'd trusted him before, but only because she had to. She and the four other captives had been at the mercy of him and his Blackfoot comrades. He'd never showed anything but kindness, though he could have been as cruel as he wanted.

In truth, his companions had goaded and jeered at him for his gentle actions. *Weak*, they'd called him. Though this man didn't possess a scrap of weakness. His height, the breadth of his shoulders tapering to a lean waist, all wrapped in sinewy muscles. The buckskin tunic and leggings he wore disguised none of his strength.

No, the man wasn't weak.

But could he be trusted? As before, she was at his mercy now. Though she could try to run, her cumbersome body wouldn't take her far if he really tried to catch her. Better she stand and face him like a woman of strength.

Grasping trunks on both sides of her, she did her best to pull herself up with more grace than she could usually manage these days. The weight of her belly tugged her, and she braced her feet as she turned to face the man.

She was downhill from him now, at least a dozen steps away. With him positioned so much higher than she, he looked as large as a grizzly standing on its back legs, pawing the air.

Maybe he realized the fear his position might plant in her, for he started walking downhill. Not directly to her, but a little sideways. When he reached the same level as her, he came to a stop with about five steps separating them.

She could see his face well now, the earnest expression marking his handsome features. He looked almost...worried.

He motioned toward her belly. "Are you well?" His brows rose in question.

She cradled the swell, her hand finding its usual place to support the babe. Even before, he'd seemed worried about the child inside her, taking extra care with her and stepping in when the others grew rough in their treatment. His gentleness hadn't won him any favors with the other braves, and she'd been so grateful for his kindness. Grateful enough to ensure her sister and the others spared his life when they came to rescue her.

In answer to his questioning gaze, she nodded. "The babe is well. It will be coming soon." Did Chogan understand her? He'd spoken four times now in her language, so maybe he'd learned more than he knew before. His eyes showed understanding.

If so, it was time he answer a question for her. She lifted her chin. "Why have you come?"

His gaze narrowed, not in animosity but as if he were trying to decide something. Maybe deciphering her words in his mind. Just in case, she asked the question again using the common language of signs all the tribes understood.

He still hesitated. Trying to decide what to say? Or attempting to find Nimiipuu words to speak it? Would he tell the truth? Did he have reason to lie? That would depend on his motive.

At last, he leveled his chin, holding her gaze with directness in his own. "My people have sent me away. I've journeyed a full moon through the mountains, asking the great spirit to show me my purpose. I did not realize how far I'd come. But I now see he's led me to you."

She worked to take in his words. Though he stumbled through some of them, he spoke her language. Had he known it all along? Why had he hidden his understanding from her before? Maybe that was how he'd known she was with child, even though she'd taken pains to wear clothing that wouldn't reveal her condition. But perhaps he'd overheard her speaking to the other captives of the babe. She'd assumed it was the one time she'd rested her hand on her belly that gave her away. He'd been watching and had given her a look of full understanding. But maybe he'd known before that.

Forcing her focus back to the present, she studied him as she mulled through his words. "Why did your people send you away?" Surely it didn't have to do with his kindness during their kidnapping.

The sadness that had cloaked his gaze before grew thicker now, confirming her fear. She gripped the tree harder as words tumbled out of her. "Because of me? Us?"

He shook his head once. "I have never agreed with my people's desire for war. That campaign was my last chance to be the man of bloodshed my father would have me be. I will not go against how I feel here." He pressed a fist to his chest. "I do not regret helping you." He lifted his chin. "I know my place is not with people of war. I have been following the great spirit's leading to show me what he would have me do."

A swirl of conflicting emotions tangled in her chest. Chogan was here. What would her family say? Her brothers couldn't even speak the word *Blackfoot* without spitting. Yet he'd been so kind to her in those fearful days of the kidnapping last winter. Now he'd been cast out from his village for his actions.

And he spoke of the great spirit's leading. She'd never questioned the beliefs she'd been taught from her earliest days, but

7

her sister Meksem had been speaking to her of the God Meksem now served. A God stronger than the great spirit. A God who made every person and thing that existed, with all power, far more than the sun or any other being. Yet Meksem said this God cared about every part of her life, wanted good for her, and was guiding her to that good path, even through the hard times.

If the great spirit had led Chogan here, did Meksem's God have any part in it? And why here, to a quiet Nimiipuu village with good cause to hate the Blackfoot?

Chogan wouldn't know of her husband's passing. The last time she'd seen this man, Heinmot had been alive, and she'd not even known how bad his sickness had progressed. A pang pressed her chest.

Should she speak of him? She didn't want this man to think she was asking for help.

She wasn't. In truth, her family had been kind to take her back into their lodge. No matter how much she felt like a stranger amidst the cluster of bodies and heat and smoke that nearly suffocated her.

Chogan must have seen something of her thoughts on her face. He certainly watched her closely enough. "Your brave, he is recovered?"

Had she spoken of Heinmot to this man? They'd communicated mostly through signs before. Chogan must have overheard her speaking with one of the other women who had been taken with her.

She narrowed her gaze at him. "You know our language."

A sheepish grin slipped over his face, and he shrugged. His actions more than confirmed the truth of her words.

Anger slid through her. Why had he lied about his understanding? He'd never actually *said* he didn't speak their language. But his face had never revealed comprehension when they spoke to him in Nimiipuu. That naturally made her assume.

Again, he seemed to read her thoughts, for his brows dipped as his gaze turned earnest. Troubled. "I did not want my brothers to know I could speak your language. I did not want them to make me use that against you. I also knew if they heard me speaking much with you that they couldn't understand, they would become angry and not believe what I told them you said."

She studied him as she took in his reasons. This time, she was careful to let her face show only distrust. At least until she was sure whether she *could* trust him or not. "Why wouldn't they believe you? You were one of them." But not anymore? Could she dare believe what he said now? She might have been more willing before learning that he'd lied about their language.

His hand cut through the air. "They have long been displeased with me. This was my last chance to show myself as bloodthirsty as the rest of them."

Nothing in his face made her think he was lying, but it took more than a few words to prove a man's true character. Still, she would be civil to him as long as he did the same.

She gave him a nod, which wouldn't commit her one way or another—she hoped.

He seemed to accept the response. "Is your brave recovered?"

She'd been distracted before and hadn't answered him. She would speak the truth now. It was what she wanted from him, so she should do the same. "He has been gone these four moons."

Chogan's expression shifted. Softened. His brows drew close again, and his eyes glistened. "I'm sorry."

Was he? About the death of a Salish man, the known enemies of the Blackfoot?

But whether everything he said now was true or not, Chogan had already proved himself different from the others who'd kidnapped her. Why would he feign sadness now if he didn't feel it?

Again, she nodded to acknowledge his words.

His gaze dropped to her belly, then lifted again to her face. "His family has taken you in?"

Maybe that was the way his people handled such matters, but thankfully, she'd been allowed to return to her own family. She shook her head. "I have come back to the village of my people. To the lodge of my brother."

Curiosity flickered in his gaze, but then it slipped away. "Do you need anything? Have your men found enough hunting? I can bring you meat."

Again, a jumble of emotions churned through her. Why would he offer more kindness? Did he truly think the great spirit brought him here to help her? Meat wasn't what she needed. And what she did long for was certainly not something she could seek from him.

Her own life again, free from the pressure to wed a man she couldn't even bring herself to like.

It didn't even have to be the life she'd thought would be hers for the rest of her days—to keep the lodge for Heinmot until he grew old and passed away. By then, their future sons would have grown enough to provide for her. She'd not expected it to all end so soon, before even the first of those children had the chance to see the world. If only this coming baby could have met his or her father.

She pushed those thoughts away lest Chogan decipher them on her face. "We have enough meat. I am well." Hot, weary, and as large as a community lodge, but he could help with none of those.

It was time she end this unusual meeting. Her family would worry if she didn't return soon.

Before turning away, Telípe sought out Chogan's gaze one last time. "I must go now. You will not stay in this place?" Surely he knew what an uproar would be raised if a Blackfoot warrior was found hiding in the woods outside their village.

Chogan's eyes drilled into hers. "I will not leave yet, not until I know the great spirit's purpose for me."

Another press of fear weighed her chest. "If they find you, they'll not wait to ask your purpose. My people detest the Blackfoot." *Hate* would have been a more accurate word, but she couldn't bring herself to say it. Not about him.

His expression remained calm, though still intense. "I won't be found. And I won't do harm to your people. You may tell them so, if you think it wise."

She shook her head. "They would hunt you down if they knew you were here."

"I won't be found." He repeated the words in a steady tone with a peace that belied the determination in their meaning.

He was such a mystery, this man. Enemy, yet friend. Fierce warrior, yet gentle and kind. Undecided, yet determined.

Well, he would have to make his own choices. If she stayed away much longer, one of the boys would be sent to find her. Or worse yet, Pisákas, the man her brother seemed determine she marry. If Chogan were spotted, she'd be putting him at great risk.

"I must go." With a final nod, she turned away.

She'd once thought she'd never see this man again. Yet she'd been granted one more chance. Was this now their final farewell?

And why did the thought make her chest ache?

CHAPTER 2

*D*espite the whirlwind of thoughts within him, Chogan held himself motionless. But his gaze tracked the woman until she disappeared through the trees.

Even as he'd neared the western edge of the mountains, Telípe had been on his mind. Honestly, she'd never wandered far from his thoughts—not since that first instant he saw her, when he and the others captured the women and child that awful day. He'd hated every moment he'd been required to keep her bound.

But when her sister and the other warriors—one Blackfoot among so many white men—arrived to free the prisoners, watching Telípe ride away—out of his life—had been hard in a very different way.

When he was exiled with no option to return to his father's village, he couldn't bring himself to travel any direction except west. Toward Telípe's village. But a few days into his journey, he'd realized he couldn't see her again. She was married. He had no right to her, even to observe her from a distance. She belonged to another man.

So he'd adjusted his route southward, toward the river he'd

heard flowed all the way to the great water. He'd never expected to find Telípe *here*. Her home must be at least a day's ride to the north, maybe longer.

Now, he understood why the great spirit had brought him to this place.

Telípe no longer belonged to another. He *could* see her. Though he might never be worthy of her, at least he might be able to help her. With the birth of her child growing near, he would provide for her in every way he could.

She was long gone now, so he turned back up the slope to gather his wits. He'd not planned to camp for the night yet. He'd merely been traveling downhill through the trees when he heard the sounds of something heavy tromping through the leaves. The bear he'd seen three sleeps before had made a similar noise, so he'd hoisted himself up in the tree before the creature could spot him.

He never expected the source of the sound to be an Indian woman heavy with child. And certainly not Telípe.

But her presence here meant he would stay for now. The rocky area he'd passed a little way back might be the best place to camp. He'd spotted a few overhangs that would keep him dry and hold in the heat from his campfire. The place would also be far enough from where her people must be camped—they weren't likely to trek that far—yet close enough he could reach her with supplies.

Unless her people knew the place, maybe as a special ceremonial or hunting ground? He'd have to watch for signs of frequent use.

Starting along his backtrail, he relished the strain in his limbs from climbing the hills. His father had sent him away without a horse or gun, stripping away the two possessions prized most by the warriors. Chogan had recognized the shame he was supposed to feel.

Yet how could he feel shame in kindness? In showing

decency to people weaker than himself? He didn't regret his actions toward Telípe and the other captives. Not even expelling him without his musket could make him wish he'd treated her differently.

He missed Kiááyo, the mount who'd served him faithfully for several years. Though the first few days hiking through the mountains on foot had been exhausting, the effort had given him a new strength he never would've possessed otherwise. His muscles grew stronger, his feet tougher. Whatever quest lay before him, the journey prepared him to face it.

When the ground leveled off, he shifted into a run, something he'd been doing more of late to build his stamina. At the faster pace, the section of rocky ground approached quickly. This area appeared different than the rest, the stone almost black in some places and sandy in others. Perhaps a fire had roared through here long ago, the flame hot enough to scorch not only the trees but the mountain itself.

Slowing, he circled the area, which expanded wider than he'd first suspected. The overhangs he'd spotted would suffice for a camp. Both extended long enough for him to stretch out, although the areas were easily seen by anyone who traveled through here. He needed to find a more concealed location.

Finally, he stumbled on the perfect spot. Actually stumbled, as his foot broke through a piece of thin flaky stone.

The stone served as a ceiling over what looked like a low cave. Other animals, or maybe weather, had chipped away the ceiling in several places, including the hole he'd forged with his foot.

Inside, the ceiling rose barely tall enough for him to sit upright. The openings in the roof would allow smoke to vent from his campfire, and there was a larger gap where he could enter. This would work.

Before he set up his camp, he decided to finish scouting the area, lest there be any other surprises—perhaps not as desirable. He found no sign of people traveling through here recently except the few prints his own feet had made. Several piles of animal droppings littered the ground, appearing to be from goat and bighorn sheep.

Then something else caught his eye. He almost missed it as his mind had already moved ahead to how he would set up his camp.

Yet there the sign lay. Chogan knelt beside the paw print, stretching his hand out beside it, though not touching the stone lest he leave a mark too. The track spread almost the size of his hand with fingers fully extended.

Chills pricked his arms. A mountain cat. A male, though probably just reaching the age to establish its own territory. Chogan had only seen tracks of two full grown male cats, and one of those he'd seen in person, its lifeless body stretched out over the horse's rump after his father's successful hunt. Those massive paws had been even wider than his father's stretched hand.

Shifting his focus, he scanned the area farther around. The animal had been moving from the woods toward the center of this black stone area, but it seemed to rub the mud off its foot with this single step, not leaving any tracks farther in. When he had a spare moment, he would search for other signs. For now, he'd best set up camp before darkness fell.

The low cave proved perfect for him to sleep, small enough to warm easily, and contained enough to hold the heat all through the night. He started a fire as dusk settled, then he gathered enough pine needles for a soft bed and laid a fur over them.

As he sank onto the pallet to eat his meal, a cry rose up in the distance. The hairs on his neck stood on end, and a shiver ran down his spine. The sound registered almost like a woman's scream—yet the tone held enough wildness that it had to be the scream of a mountain cat.

Then the cry deepened. It was cut short as another feral scream echoed. This one still sounded like a wildcat, yet possessed a different tenor.

He reached for the knife hanging at his neck, though the sounds were distant. The dueling cats were too far away to be a danger to him now, but he'd need to stay on his guard. The animal that wasn't chased away this night would consider this his territory from now on.

Telípe.

His pulse sped to a gallop. Had either animal approached near enough her camp to be a danger? When he rose in the morning, he would go to the place the mountain cats fought and follow their prints. Then he would seek out Telípe's village and see if her people lived within the region the cat would claim as his own.

Perhaps Chogan's first offering of meat to this woman might be the tender flesh of a wildcat. He would ensure not only her belly stayed filled, but her home remained safe.

～

Telípe could feel her sister's gaze on her as they walked, but she kept her own focus resolutely ahead. When she'd mentioned her plan to pick berries again today, Ámtiz's grandmother had eyed the bulk of Telípe's belly with a frown. It shouldn't have surprised her that before she even reached the outer edge of the village, her sister Meksem caught up with her, her own basket in hand.

She couldn't remember the last time she and Meksem had gone berry picking together. Maybe back when Telípe was ten or eleven summers old, around the time Meksem had fully focused her efforts on training with the other warriors. Since those days, a tomahawk seemed to fit so much better in Meksem's hand than a basket. The fact that her sister would do so now brought a smile to Telípe's weary mouth, an expression harder and harder to manage of late.

The only problem with Meksem accompanying her was that she'd planned to pick in the same area where she'd seen Chogan the other day. Surely he wouldn't be there still. If he had any wisdom at all, he'd be halfway back across the mountains by now. Or trekking alongside the westward river as he'd planned to do.

She'd thought of him so often since that day. When her feet started this way, she didn't have the strength to resist the longing to see him once more.

What was it about that man that drew her? During the kidnapping, she'd been grateful for his kindness, so worried for her babe that his attention had swept through her with relief.

Then after Meksem and her friends freed Telípe and she learned of Heinmot's sickness, a new fear had emerged. Though her husband had been older than her by more than fifteen summers, he'd been kind. She'd been content with their life together. The thought of losing that life—of losing him—had flared worry that she'd tried to press down as she cared for him in his final days. The friendship that had grown between them strengthened during that time, even as his own life waned.

She'd mourned Heinmot these last four moons—the good man, the friend he'd been. She would continue to mourn him, but the birth looming before her consumed most of her thoughts.

Except these last few days, Chogan had taken over some of them.

As she and Meksem reached the edge of the trees and the base of the hill, Telípe pointed toward the chokecherry bushes. "Let's see if more berries are ripe."

Meksem glanced at the brush, then swept her gaze around

the woods as they walked. Maybe bringing Meksem here was a mistake. Her warrior instincts made her far too likely to spot Chogan's presence if he hid in the same spot.

But he wouldn't. He had no reason to come back to this place to wait for her.

She still couldn't quite believe he'd been there once. His presence probably had nothing to do with her. He wouldn't have even expected her to be in this village.

She reached for a tree to help her up the hill as her steps slowed and her breathing grew harder. Meksem noticed and grabbed Telípe's elbow to help.

She would have sent her sister a thankful smile, but breathing and trudging uphill took everything she could manage. Every step came slower.

At last, Meksem tugged her to a stop. "Sit here and rest. I'll see if there are any berries ready to be picked."

She didn't have the breath to argue nor resist when her sister helped her to sit on the leaf-strewn ground.

While Meksem moved on to the berry bushes, Telípe rested a hand where the babe poked a bony limb against her side. The child hadn't been as active the past few days. Likely, there wasn't enough room to move around. She focused on drawing in breath, lifting her chest and shoulders with each inhale.

At last, her heart began to slow to a more normal pace and her chest didn't ache from lack of breath. Maybe the grandmother was right to worry. But these berry picking walks provided her only chance to clear her head from the chaos in the lodge.

She glanced over at Meksem, who bent low to pick from a section Telípe must have missed before. No surprise, for her belly blocked the view of anything around her feet.

Against her better judgment, her gaze lifted to the tree where she'd first spotted Chogan. That had been an excellent hiding spot, for its leaves were thicker than most of the trees around. And the faint bits of bark that could be seen between the greenery were the exact color of buckskins. She squinted as the brown shifted.

Could it be? The dark color moved again, and the whites of a pair of eyes took shape. Then the flash of teeth in a grin.

She barely held in a squeal as she pressed a hand to her chest to contain the excitement thrumming there. He was here. Again.

She pressed her lips tight, though her smile still tugged at her mouth. She could make out his features much better now that she knew what she was looking at, and she couldn't miss the laughter in his eyes. She'd never seen him smile like that, and the sight sent a flutter all the way through her.

She'd best not show her reaction though, in case Meksem looked her way. In truth, if Chogan made even a tiny sound, Meksem would hear and jerk him down to press a knife to his throat before the man could take a breath.

Maybe he didn't realize how keen her sister's instincts were. He'd met Meksem during the rescue, had nearly been plunged through by her blade. Telípe had stood in the way—the only thing that held her sister off. But now Telípe could never get up quickly enough to place herself between them.

She squinted at the man to give him warning with her gaze, then flicked her focus to Meksem.

His face turned solemn, and he gave a single nod. He didn't move again, just sat there watching her.

For her own part, Telípe could barely keep from fidgeting. Any moment, Meksem would look up and see him. Her sister had an uncanny knack for sensing an intruder. He didn't even have to make a sound. She would know.

Telípe couldn't wait for that to happen. She had to distract Meksem before she had a chance to notice him.

Lumbering up to her hands and knees, she called out, "I just remembered another place that has the best elderberries. If we don't get them now, they may be overripe soon."

Meksem reached her side by the time Telípe straightened to her knees and grabbed a tree to help pull herself up. She hated being this large and clumsy, especially in front of anyone else. Especially Chogan. But she hadn't been able to stand without something to clutch for almost the length of a moon.

Meksem hung by her side like a worried mother duck as Telípe waddled down the tree-covered hillside. Maybe she could get her sister to go ahead so she could have a moment to speak with Chogan. She had to convince him to leave this place before something bad happened to him.

When they neared the base of the hill and the edge of the woods, Telípe slowed and braced a hand under her belly. She didn't even have to feign exhaustion as she motioned Meksem forward. "You go on and see if any berries are left. I'll sit here in the sunshine and rest until you return."

Meksem studied her, brows lowered. "Perhaps we should go back now."

Telípe gave her the most pleading look she could manage. "Not yet. I can't suffer being inside that dark smoky lodge." She reached for a tree to lower herself to the ground. Once she was down, Meksem wouldn't make her get up again so soon.

After settling on the leaves, she sent her sister as contented a look as she could manage. "Go. I don't want to waste those berries. Come back for me when you're done. You know the place they'll be, right?" Telípe pointed around the base of the low mountain to the right. "It's just around that curve in a thicket."

Meksem glanced that way, probably debating the merits of leaving Telípe by herself. She finally nodded. "I won't be long. Call out if you need me."

"Take your time. The sun feels wonderful, I might even sleep a while." She eased back against the tree behind her. The knobby trunk didn't offer much comfort, but at least she didn't have to hold herself upright.

"Rest then." The gentle note in Meksem's tone sent a twinge of guilt through Telípe.

But as her sister padded away, Telípe didn't attempt to stop her. Not with the man hiding not far away.

CHAPTER 3

Telípe listened for Chogan's approach behind her but heard nothing until his voice registered a few steps back.

"Your sister? The one who would have plunged a blade through my heart?"

Telípe glanced back at the man. His handsomeness struck her anew, and the hint of grin twitching at his mouth made it hard to hold in her own. She should be angry at him for putting himself in danger. Yet seeing him again evaporated her frustration like steam fading in the air.

"She would plunge her knife in you still if she found you here. You must leave. Why do you linger?"

Chogan's mouth sobered as he pulled a leather-wrapped bundle from his waistband. "I brought you meat. Wildcat." He leaned forward to extend the bundle for her to reach, though he stayed back far enough Meksem wouldn't be able to see him if she rounded the bend.

At the word *wildcat*, Telípe jerked her gaze to his face. "You found it alive?" They didn't have many such animals in their territory. But when one did stray near, mothers kept their children close. Wildcats were one of the only animals known to attack people without being provoked, even stalking prey and lying in wait for the perfect moment to attack. But if Chogan had killed the beast, there would be no cause for alarm this time.

Chogan nodded. "A young male. He took only two arrows to bring him down. There is another nearby though. I heard them fighting before I found this one."

Worry pressed her chest. "I'll tell my people to be careful."

His gaze intensified on her. "You be careful too. I'll hunt him. Hopefully, soon I will bring you *his* flesh for your stew pot as well. Mayhap his hide will form a nice cradleboard." A glimmer touched his gaze again.

A smile tickled her mouth. This man had a better sense of humor then she would've thought.

His gaze flicked in the direction Meksem had gone, and she glanced that way too. No sign of her sister, but she might return any minute. Shifting her focus back to Chogan, she took the meat. "Thank you for this, but are you sure you have enough to eat?"

His chin bobbed once. "One man needs little."

As much as she hated to, she had to send him away permanently this time. "You must leave this place. It's not safe for you. If my people know a Blackfoot brave is nearby, they'll hunt you. And if they learn you were one of those who…" She didn't need to finish the thought. "It's not safe for you. I may not be able to protect you this time."

His gaze softened, roaming over her face almost like a caress. "It is not for you to protect me. I will be careful, but I will not leave until my work here is done."

Frustration slipped through her, but before she could respond, his gaze again jerked toward where Meksem had gone.

Telípe followed his focus once more, and her sister appeared around the mountain, her stride purposeful as always. Telípe glanced back to make sure Chogan was leaving.

He'd already gone, disappeared completely.

Tucking the bundle of meat under the edge of her tunic, she repositioned herself as she waited for Meksem to reach her.

Meksem held the basket low for Telípe to see inside. "Most of the elderberries are gone. You're ready to return now?"

Telípe nodded, reaching for a tree to help her rise. Standing proved even more awkward this time, as she concealed the bundle of meat Chogan had given.

His gift would be a welcome addition to their stew pot, but the sooner she got her warrior sister away from this place, the better.

~

*S*urely the pains couldn't get any worse than this. Telípe knelt on her bed pallet, clutching a rolled buckskin in both hands as she squeezed her eyes against the agony wrapping around her belly.

"Breathe, my daughter. You must breathe slowly in and out. Even though it hurts." The grandmother's gentle hand rubbing across her back offered the only flicker of relief amidst the darkness of the pain.

At last, the pressure burning around her eased, and Telípe could finally take in those breaths the grandmother urged. As she sank back on her heels, their friend Elan rubbed a damp cloth over her face. The cool water soothed more than anything else had yet.

As she soaked in breaths, she glanced around the empty lodge. The grandmother had chased out everyone except herself and Elan, who'd been through childbirth before and had a calming nature that made her an excellent healer.

If Heinmot had been here, he would have been sent out too.

The men would be keeping him occupied, plying him with stories and a pipe.

But he wasn't here, and he'd never meet his child.

She had no time for sadness as another pain wrapped around her belly. She bent forward, squeezing the rolled buckskin. This time she would do better with her breathing.

But as that agony pressed through her, breath seemed impossible to manage. This pain lasted longer than the others, and when it finally gave way, her body received only a short rest before another rushed in.

And this time, a new urgency surged through her.

"Push, my daughter. The time has come to meet your babe."

~

Chogan stood at the edge of the trees, straining for every sound drifting from the Nimíipuu camp. Loneliness wrapped around him, stronger than he could ever remember the feeling. Even when he'd first been sent away, the isolation hadn't struck this hard.

Telípe was there, in the camp, in that second lodge, third from the corner, if he wasn't mistaken. He'd only come for a glimpse of the village, to show himself what he could never have. But when he'd seen all the activity around that lodge—the women ducking in and out and the men standing far enough away not to be heard—a knowing had settled deep inside him.

He'd waited, even as the sun rose higher in the sky. Then he'd heard the woman's moans, not piercing screams, but the deep groans of unfathomable pain, and he'd known. As surely as if he'd been kneeling by her side, he had no doubt Telípe's time had come.

If only he *could* be by her side.

But he could only stand here, hiding. Always just outside the circle of acceptance.

He'd hardened himself against the longing to be allowed in by his own people—by his own family especially. He didn't believe the same things they did. Why should he want to be included in what he knew to be wrong?

But Telípe. She was good. And brave. The only woman he'd ever admired.

Now in her pain, he could do nothing to help her except petition the great spirit for her safety. For the child's safety too. Would the spirit hear and grant his request? If only he had a way of knowing. A sign, or even a feeling. But his thoughts seemed to evaporate as they left his mind, never reaching the far-off being he asked to help.

When the sun reached its peak, his nerves had grown so taut he was almost willing to stride forward into the camp. Maybe they would tell him how Telípe fared before they sent an arrow through his heart.

But then a glorious sound filled the air. A lusty cry, high-pitched and urgent. The sound of a hungry babe.

Joy sluiced through him, spreading all the way to his fingers and toes. He gripped the tree he hid behind to keep himself from crying out with his own happiness. The babe was alive. And Telípe? Surely if the child lived, she did as well.

Memories tried to slip in of his brother's face when his first wife had died during childbirth. Stony and blank, a shield to cover his pain.

Chogan pushed back the image. Telípe had possessed strength even when weighed down with the babe inside her. She would come through this.

Still, fear gripped his throat, and he strained for any sound from her. He focused his gaze on that lodge so he would see and catch the expression of any woman who entered or left. He would know by their posture whether joy or sorrow reigned this day.

Another sound slipped out to him. A small mewling cry. It

had the same urgency and tone that marked that of a newborn. But this wasn't at all the lusty cry he'd heard moments before. Then that first cry sounded again, covering over the smaller sound.

Could it be...? There couldn't possibly be two, could there? Telípe's belly had been large, but every woman near childbirth grew big around.

Once the louder cry eased, he again heard the sounds of quieter mewling. Definitely a different babe. Then that one, too, grew silent.

A little while later, the flap over the lodge door opened, and a woman peered out. She wore a wide smile and motioned toward the other women who lingered outside.

As they rose and filed into the lodge, he squinted to make out any details inside the home. There was too much darkness behind the flap to see.

But that smile must have been good, right? There would be no joy if Telípe's life had ebbed during the birthing.

Finally, he let himself sink against the tree's rough bark. She was well. The babe—or babes—sounded well too. Except that one had seemed weaker than the other. If one of the children didn't make it, he could only imagine Telípe's pain.

In this, he couldn't help her either. He was powerless.

Once again, he had to look on from a distance while those he cared about suffered.

~

"*L*ook how happy she is. I think she's trying to smile." Elan raised Telípe's second born for them all to see before moving Éisnin to her shoulder to pat her back. The milk-sated baby did indeed look pleased, and the satisfied burp she gave seemed to confirm it. From the moment Telípe had first seen that almost-smile, Éisnin had been the only name that would suit. *Happy*. It described this babe well—both her own tiny personality and what she sought to bring out in others.

Telípe tucked her firstborn close as she continued to nurse. Kapskáps was the smaller of the two, so tiny she only stretched twice the length of Telípe's hand. Her cry was as small as the babe herself.

But she'd fought her way out first and now drank longer than her sister every time. Like she was determined to catch up, maybe even exceed her sister's size. She was a fighter, this one. Which was why the name that meant *Strong* seemed to fit her perfectly. Though she be small, she would do great things.

Telípe glanced over at Éisnin, settled comfortably on Elan's shoulder. That one's personality was as big as the rest of her, already winning hearts with her coos and babbles. It seemed hard to believe they could have such strong natures from the moment they entered the world—and be so different.

When Kapskáps finished her meal, Susanna reached out for the babe. The white woman's own belly expanded large with child—maybe another moon or two at the most—and she'd come often to the women's lodge to help Telípe with the newborns.

Telípe didn't speak much of the white man's tongue, but she was learning. Susanna had begun learning Nimiiputimpt, as well as a bit of sign. Together, they managed to communicate. And in truth, what need were words when these two bundles lit up the room, stealing all focus?

Elan glanced up from fussing over Éisnin and met Telípe's gaze. "Is Meksem coming to walk with you today? I'm happy to go with you if she's occupied."

Telípe looked to the lodge opening, but her sister hadn't appeared yet. Meksem had come to visit her and the babes in the women's lodge each day, and as soon as Telípe grew strong enough to walk a distance, she'd insisted they stroll in the sunshine. There always seemed to be eager hands nearby to hold the little ones, giving Telípe a few minutes of peace. The babes had stolen her heart from the first moment she saw each —in truth, long before that—but a few minutes away from them made her better. More peaceful, though the walks exhausted her. They'd been traveling farther each day, and she'd recovered her strength quickly these last times.

Footsteps sounded outside the lodge, though they couldn't be Meksem. Her sister wouldn't make so much noise as she approached. She'd worked hard, even as a child, to silence her tread. These sounded like the heavier stride of a man. Her chest tightened at the thought it might be Pisákas. He'd been away on several hunts these past days, so she'd seen blessed little of him. The one time he'd come to walk with her, she'd feigned too much exhaustion to leave the lodge. She couldn't place exactly what about the man bothered her. He didn't seem cruel or dangerous. In fact, he'd never paid her much notice at all...not until her brother had begun to encourage a union between them. The thought of wedding again only four moons after she'd buried Heinmot seemed impossible, but she could understand why Síkem would want her out of his overcrowded lodge —especially now that she'd brought forth two new hungry, fussing bodies instead of the one they'd expected.

"Elan?" Joel's voice sounded through the lodge opening, and Telípe eased out a breath of relief. Joel stayed outside, not pushing aside the flap to look in. The men usually kept a good distance from this hut set aside for women during their time of bleeding.

Elan glanced at Telípe as though for approval, probably to invite her husband to open the flap.

She nodded in response to Elan's unspoken question. Of course he could come see the babes—and his wife.

The woman turned toward the opening as she gave Éisnin another pat. "Come in, my love."

The door flap shook as Joel pulled it aside. His gaze located

Elan on the first sweep and hovered on her, his eyes turning gentle as he took in his wife holding the babe.

A familiar burn squeezed Telípe's throat, creeping up to her eyes. Would Heinmot have looked at her that way as she held one of their daughters? Maybe he'd not be as besotted as Joel seemed. And in truth, she'd never really yearned for the love that sparked between these two. That hadn't been part of her relationship with Heinmot, even though he'd been her husband.

But the tenderness in Joel's eyes...she couldn't help longing for a man she cared about to look at her that way.

Before the thought could take root, she pushed it away.

With effort, Joel seemed to tug his focus from his wife as he turned to Telípe. "One of the women found fresh tracks of a wildcat, so a few warriors have gathered a hunting party. Meksem is going with them, and she asked me to tell you she's sorry she can't take you walking today."

Though she caught enough of Joel's English words to understand his meaning, Elan spoke quietly to interpret. When she finished, she added on. "I can go with you Telípe." She glanced at Susanna, maybe to see if Susanna should come along as well. Perhaps they could bring both babes. But a look at the woman's swollen belly kept her quiet.

Telípe glanced from one friend to the other, her gaze slipping to the little ones they both held. It would be good for the babes to get fresh air too. Kapskáps was tiny enough. It wouldn't be hard for Telípe to carry her while they walked.

Yet a part of her strained against the encumbrance. These walks gave her a small bit of time to clear her mind from all the details of the wee ones. She needed this break. The time with Meksem had been refreshing, but time alone might be even more so.

She shook her head, sending Elan a smile to soften her refusal. "I'll just walk a little way by myself. It will be easier than carrying these with us."

Elan's eyes said she understood, probably comprehending more than Telípe said. She reached out and laid a gentle hand on Telípe's arm. "Enjoy yourself. Stay out as long as you like, but don't wear yourself out."

With a nod, Telípe pressed up to her feet. After a final glance at her little ones—Éisnin had already fallen asleep, and Kapskáps seemed ready to join her sister—she turned toward the lodge opening and stepped outside.

Joel motioned to the north, toward the open land that ran between the river on their left and the wooded hill to the right. "The mountain lion tracks are in the grassland that way. Better stay clear of that area."

She nodded her thanks, then headed through camp toward the woods to the east.

Surely Chogan had left the area as she told him to. But she couldn't seem to stop herself from going to the place she'd found him twice now.

Just in case he might be waiting for her again.

CHAPTER 4

$\mathcal{T}$hough Telípe no longer carried two babes within her, her body still lacked the strength she'd once possessed, a fact that came abundantly clear as she trekked across the grassy plain toward the hill where she'd met Chogan before. She managed to climb the tree-covered slope without grabbing onto a trunk with each step to pull her up. She breathed hard as she neared the tree where he'd hidden before.

She strained to see through the leaves. Only a few dark spots showed the bark behind the green. Too dark to be buckskins. Still, she stepped closer, approaching all the way to the base of the tree. No one sat among the branches, though now that she had a look into the limbs, she could see how this made the perfect hiding place. A thick branch sat at just the right height for a tall man like Chogan to lift himself up. And the leaves created an excellent barrier to hide him.

"Telípe."

She spun at his voice, her heart leaping in a mixture of surprise and joy.

Chogan stood a few paces up the hill, looking as strong and handsome as ever. Somehow, when she wasn't with him, her mind forgot how striking he was, how broad his shoulders stretched, and how perfectly his features fit together.

Now, her heart no longer pounded from surprise, only from the attraction raised by his nearness.

He stepped closer, and the act did nothing to slow her pulse. She clutched the tree beside her for strength—for steadiness— as he approached to only the length of two arms away.

His gaze roamed her face as if checking for anything amiss. He seemed almost hungry for whatever news her expression might offer. "You're well?"

Realization swept through her. He wouldn't know about Kapskáps and Éisnin yet. Her eyes slipped down to her belly, flatter than before but nowhere near as slim as she'd once been. At least he would see the obvious, but he wouldn't know that overlarge baby had actually been two.

She looked back up at him, the joy of her news spreading across her face. "It was two. Two girls."

"Girls." His grin lit his face and eyes and every part of him as though he were nearly as happy at the idea as she was. Then his brows notched. "They're well?"

She nodded. "They're beautiful. Kapskáps was firstborn, and she's tiny but has more spunk than any babe I've seen. She's determined to catch up with her sister, I think. Éisnin already has rolls on her hands and loves to bring a smile to everyone."

If anything, Chogan's grin widened. He shook his head, seeming awed by the surprising news. "Two girls."

Watching his pleasure doubled her own. For some strange reason, his pleasure soothed some of the ache of giving birth without Heinmot there to see his children.

Then his eyes gentled as his gaze swept over her face again. "And you? You are well?" The same question as before, but this time sorrow blanketed his features. "I listened from the trees. I heard the pain."

His eyes added an unspoken *I'm sorry*. Almost as if her agonized cries had brought him pain too.

She nodded. "It's done." Though she would always remember the agony of that day. "The girls are well and worth it all."

He nodded, but his brow still gathered. Perhaps he would understand if he saw the babes.

A new longing flared inside her, and she gave it voice before she allowed herself time to push the idea away. "I'd like you to meet them."

The moment the words left her mouth, their foolishness swept through her. Heat flared up her neck. Why would this great warrior wish to meet two scrappy newborns? And girls, at that.

She pulled back, tucking closer to the tree and wishing she could hide behind its bark. "I mean, if you're around when I bring them for a walk, you can see them. If you wish."

He regarded her with a look she couldn't quite decipher. Amusement? Not like he was laughing at her. At least, she hoped not. But something else tinged the expression. Hope? Longing? She couldn't tell for sure.

After several heartbeats, he finally spoke. "I do wish to see them." In the breath of silence that came next, he must have been coming to the same reality she had. If only she could take him back to the village now, walk him on the path between the lodges. Take her children from Elan and Susanna and present them to this man. If only this giant rift didn't exist between their peoples.

His next words came tentatively. "Can you bring them out? Meet me at the edge of the trees?" He pointed toward the base of the hill they stood on.

She didn't need long to consider the idea before she nodded. She no longer belonged to a man or anyone else who had command over her. If she wanted to bring her children for a walk, she could.

"When?" Hope gave Chogan's voice an undertone of urgency.

Bringing both babies this far would not be easy with her weakened body. But she was gaining strength every day. "Two sleeps from now, when the sun reaches the high point."

Pleasure slipped across Chogan's face. "I look forward to it."

She needed to get back before someone came looking for her, but she had to ask once more. "What are you doing here, Chogan?" She studied his eyes for what he might not be ready or able to say.

He met her gaze. "I'm still waiting to find out."

Then he jerked his attention toward the bottom of the hill as if he'd heard something. "Go and rest. I'll see you again soon."

~

*A*s Chogan watched Telípe pick her way down the hill, that now familiar weight tightened his chest.

Maybe he should leave, as she clearly thought best. She'd not spoken those words again this time. But she had before. What she *had* said still echoed through him.

What are you doing here, Chogan?

If only he knew the answer. He'd had nowhere to go when he left his father's village, and west had seemed like the best option. He'd even tried to avoid the town where he thought she lived. But now he knew—he'd been led here. And he wouldn't leave until he'd accomplished the spirit's purpose.

If only that purpose could include the woman who took a little piece of him each time he watched her walk away. But that could never be, not unless she chose to leave her people and come with him.

Yet now she had not one but two babes depending on her. All three of them deserved a home and the love of family gathered around them. He could give her none of that, no matter how much he longed to.

Turning uphill, he trudged toward the black stone area that was the closest thing to a home he could now claim. He couldn't muster enough strength to jog back. In truth, just pulling himself up the hill took most of what he had left. He blinked to clear his vision, which had been showing him double most of the day. Why was his body growing weaker? Was this a sign? Maybe his great trial lay ahead.

I am willing. Show me what I am to do.

But by the time he stumbled onto the dark colored stone, he couldn't have slain a mosquito if it landed on his hand. He barely tripped down into his cave, then crawled the final distance to his mat. Maybe after sleep, he would regain enough strength for whatever lay ahead.

~

*T*he scream jerked Telípe from the light sleep she'd fallen into while the babes rested.

She sat up, blinking to orient herself. Light shone in through the smoke opening at the top of the lodge and around the edges of the door flap. It must be midmorning still, for she couldn't have slept long. The babes almost never napped at the same time, but they'd all had a weary night, so she'd sunk onto her fur while the twins slept.

Another wail sounded from outside, maybe at the other end of the village.

A child. His cries increased in volume as though his pain worsened with each hiccupping breath. What had happened?

Easing away from the bed pallet, she pushed up to her feet and padded to the lodge opening. When she slipped outside, she had to squint against the bright midday sun. She raised a hand to shield her eyes as she peered in the direction of the sounds.

A group of people clustered outside a lodge, but she couldn't tell what was in the midst of them. It must be the child, whose frantic wails raised the small hairs on her arms.

Had the young one fallen from a horse? Or maybe tumbled from a tree. The child sounded young, perhaps only two or three summers old.

Sounds from inside her own lodge brought her focus there with a cringe. The tumult down the path had awakened at least one of her daughters, and the other wouldn't be long for sleep with all the noise.

Maybe she could carry them with her to see what had happened. Her bleeding had nearly stopped, so she was venturing out of the women's lodge more often than before.

Since her daughters had nursed just before they'd all settled for a nap, they shouldn't be hungry yet. Éisnin must have awakened first, for her lusty cries filled the lodge. For such a sweet-mannered infant, she possessed a powerful voice.

Telípe lifted Éisnin to her shoulder and bounced a little to soothe her as the other babe stretched and opened her dark eyes to fix them on Telípe.

Warmth slipped through her chest as she smiled at the child. "Hello, my firstborn. Shall we go see what the commotion is about?"

She'd not managed to carry both children in her arms at once, at least not in a way where she felt they were both safe. So she strapped Éisnin in the cradleboard and lifted it to her back, then stood and bent to lift the smaller babe in her arms.

Éisnin's larger size fit better in the board, and she seemed content to stare at out at the world around her. With her lighter weight, Kapskáps was easier to hold in her arms, though she seemed to grow heavier each day in a determined bid to catch up with her younger sister. Telípe had a feeling these two might always be competing, at least in Kapskáps's mind.

Once she had both little ones positioned and they stepped

into the bright sunlight, Telípe focused on the gathering where the child's cries could still be heard. The sounds were more muted now, which likely meant he'd been taken inside a lodge to be cared for. His injuries must be significant for him to still be in tears.

When she neared enough to see through the sun's glare and distinguish individual people, Meksem was the first figure she recognized.

Her sister stood at the outer edge of the gathering like a sentry standing guard. Meksem didn't usually stand around to learn gossip, so her presence here either meant the child was one of their family—maybe one of their little brothers—or maybe Meksem had helped him during the injury.

Telípe lengthened her stride to reach her sister as she glanced around the rest of the group. Adam, Meksem's husband, and his brother, Joel, stood nearby. Elan wasn't with Joel, so maybe she'd gone into the lodge to help with the child. She was becoming known for her gentle ministrations and healing touch. A few of the others from their group also stood in the cluster—Beaver Tail, French, Colette, and Louis, the younger of the two who'd come with Colette.

At last, Telípe reached Meksem. The boy's sobs had eased to occasional whimpers, though still loud enough to be heard through the skins of the lodge.

Her sister met her look with a grim expression.

"What's happened?" Telípe grabbed Meksem's arm to pull the answer from her faster.

"The wildcat we've been tracking found a group of children before we caught up to him. I reached him right after he'd sprung on the chief's nephew. He's injured, but I don't think it's as bad as it could have been."

Fear washed through her as she took in the story. That young boy had been attacked by a mountain cat? She'd seen deer carcasses mangled by those terrible claws and had once helped tend a horse that had barely escaped with its life after a wildcat attacked.

But a sweet, innocent boy…

Realization fluttered through her. Chogan had warned her about the animal. She should have told the others of his alert, but she'd been worried about how she would explain her knowledge. When Joel said Meksem and some the braves went out the day before to hunt him, she'd assumed that would be the end. Meksem always accomplished what she set her aim to. "So when you and the others went out yesterday…"

Pain grooved the outer edges of Meksem's eyes. "We tracked him until darkness, then found the trail again when the sun woke this morning. We found him too late."

Pain pressed on Telípe's chest, though maybe not as much as her sister carried. Meksem would take the weight of guilt for this boy's injuries onto herself.

Kapskáps squirmed in her arms, and she bounced a little to quiet the babe. It was her sister who needed reassurance the most right now. Telípe met her pain-filled gaze. "It's not your fault. At least the cat's dead now, right?"

Anger slipped in to cover the pain in Meksem's gaze. Her jaw tightened, and she bit her words through clenched teeth. "My arrow struck his neck, but not deep enough to draw blood. The others still chase him. I carried the lad to his mother."

Once again, a tingle ran through Telípe. The cat still lived. But surely the warriors would catch him soon. Even as quick and wily as mountain cats were known to be, the braves would outsmart him. "Maybe they've reached him by now."

Meksem didn't answer, but her lips pressed in a tight line, and her gaze shifted to the lodge where only the murmur of low adult voices now sounded.

No wonder she stood guard. Both to keep danger out and to await news from within.

Telípe dared a final question. "Do you want to go in and

help?" Meksem had never been comfortable with tasks that required a gentle touch, though she could creep quietly enough for even the faintest sounds to be muffled. She was capable of caring for an injury, but she didn't always trust her own abilities.

She gave a single shake of her head. "Elan and the boy's mother are there. I would only be in the way."

She might be right about that. Telípe would be of no help either, with her hands full of babies. Better to be here with her sister as long as the little ones would allow her.

Meksem might need the support as much as the boy and his family.

CHAPTER 5

*T*oday was the day. She would take the babes to meet Chogan.

But with so much fear creeping through the village about the wildcat, could Telípe manage to get away with her daughters? Without anyone else accompanying her as guard?

The warriors still hunted the predator, a different group this time, for the others had searched to the point of exhaustion. Meksem accompanied this new band of braves. Telípe had a feeling her sister wouldn't give up until the cat's massive hide hung suspended from a drying rack.

By all accounts, this mountain beast was the largest any of them had seen. She would have chalked the brow-raising descriptions up to tale-bearing if the words hadn't come from Meksem herself.

He was twice the length of the lad, taller than a man as he sprang onto the boy.

A new shiver slipped through her as she wrapped Kapskáps for their walk to meet Chogan. Elan had gone with Otskai to attend to the injured boy, though she'd said he was faring well.

The multiple distractions in the village might give Telípe a better chance to slip away unnoticed. Susanna and Colette had both come that morning to help her care for her babes. Both women were expecting, though Colette appeared to be a little behind Susanna. Despite the fact she spoke very little Nimiiputimpt and even less sign language, Colette possessed a caring that ran deep in her gaze.

Thankfully, both of the white women had left a little while back when she'd lain down with the babes. If they returned while she was gone, surely they would think she'd left for a walk in her daily habit. Would they worry about her since the wildcat was still on the loose? Her brother, Síkem, had said that morning that the tracks led to the other side of the river, and she would be traveling the opposite direction, toward the mountains to the east.

With Éisnin strapped in the cradleboard, Telípe pulled the carrier onto her back, then scooped up Kapskáps and stepped to the lodge opening. A glance outside showed most of the village was quiet, as often happened during the sun's peak. The youngest children would be napping and their mothers scraping hides or doing other quiet work while they had a moment to themselves.

She slipped out and around to the back of the teepee. One of the grandmothers sitting outside a lodge lifted a hand in greeting. "This sun is good for all—old and young alike."

Telípe nodded and offered a smile. "I have not seen enough of it these past days."

The woman's face grooved in a toothy grin, and she nodded agreement.

Contentment slipped through Telípe as she passed the older woman. She'd been away from these people too long. She'd not minded moving to Heinmot's village, but being back among those who knew her from her youngest days felt right.

She reached the edge of the camp without meeting anyone else and eased out a breath of relief. Now she had to travel a stretch of grassland before she reached the trees at the base of the hill. Hopefully, no one would see her and call out over the distance.

Doing her best to keep her stride casual, she focused on enjoying the sun's warm rays on her face. Yet, by the time she reached the trees, the warmth had raised moisture across her brow, and her legs threatened to give way beneath her. Kapskáps and Éisnin seemed to enjoy the warmth, or else the brightness itself kept them quiet. Neither of her children made a sound, even when she climbed a few strides up the hill to the deeper tree cover and sank to the ground to wait.

Chogan wasn't standing there waiting for her, but she shouldn't have expected him to be. He would come to her when he'd made sure no one else was around.

She positioned herself so she would see him approach. The man seemed to surprise her every time, though, and this time might be no different. Still, she'd like a chance to feast her eyes on him before he drew near enough to see the admiration in her gaze.

Yet Chogan didn't appear.

When Éisnin grew fussy in the cradleboard, Telípe laid Kapskáps down, swaddled in a light blanket, and pulled the board from her back to unstrap the younger babe. "Hello, my sweet. Do you wonder why we're not moving?"

As soon as Telípe freed Éisnin's hands, the child lifted one as though reaching out to her mother's face. Telípe leaned close and kissed the pudgy fingers. Éisnin gave her a look so near a smile, a wash of love spread through her.

She reached for the infant's other hand and pressed a kiss. "I love you, too, sweet one."

Then she turned to the other babe squirming in her blanket. She took up one of Kapskáps's hands, the fingers so much smaller than her sister's. "And I love you, my fighter." She kissed the first tiny hand, then the other.

For a while, she played with the babes, raising her gaze every so often up the hill in search of Chogan. They had said they'd meet when the sun reached its peak, right? A glance to the sky showed that point had definitely come, and the great orb was beginning its westward descent. Could something have delayed him?

A frisson of fear slipped through her. Surely the cat...

She swept the thought away as soon as it attacked. Chogan was strong and wise in the ways of animals. He knew about the creature—he'd been the one to warn her, after all.

Maybe she'd heard him wrong about today's meeting. As foggy as her mind was at times from lack of sleep, that must be what happened.

Or maybe... Had someone followed her out here? Pisákas always turned up at moments she least wanted to see him, but he'd gone with her brother on the hunt for the wildcat. She sent her gaze downhill instead of up, sweeping around the grassland visible through the trees. No one stood out there that she could see. She brought her focus nearer, to each of the trunks around her. Maybe Chogan saw something she didn't, and that's why he hadn't made his presence known.

Kapskáps began to fuss, her tiny face twisting as it always did when she cried. She must be getting hungry.

Telípe reached for Éisnin and slipped her back into the cradleboard, then laced the thongs to secure her in place.

If she didn't start back now, Kapskáps's cries would come in earnest before they reached the women's lodge.

As she gathered up her children and stood, she sent another searching look around the place. If Chogan were watching, he would at least have known she came with the children. Maybe she could try again tomorrow, and this time she would be more careful to slip away alone.

∾

*C*hogan huddled tighter under his furs, his body racking with shivers. He'd piled every cover he had over himself, even the ones he'd been sleeping atop before. He should go gather more firewood, but the heat burning through his body had stolen the strength from his limbs. The one time he'd crawled across the cave to retrieve another bundle of smoked meat had taken everything he had left.

Was this how he would die? Was this battle the one intended for him? If so, he'd proved to be a weak fighter. Maybe he really was as incapable as his father thought. The man had never used that word exactly, but his eyes had said it for him. And maybe he'd been right.

As Chogan lay there, the shivers too violent to allow him sleep, a host of memories swept through him. Images of his mother and the sister who'd died before she grew as high as his waist. His two brothers, great warriors both, with strings of scalp locks to prove it. Every time the worst of the memories resurrected, he reached for the one that soothed the churning inside him.

Telípe.

How many days had it been since he'd last met her in the woods? Had she come with her babes to meet him again? If so, he'd disappointed her. Just like he'd disappointed everyone else.

But this time, it hadn't been his choice. *I would have been there if I could...* What was the word in her language? *Hetéu. My love.* He wouldn't have the chance to tell her now, not that he would have said that final phrase anyway. It would be more than she was ready to hear.

If only he didn't have to leave her wondering why he hadn't come as they'd agreed. Maybe she would think he'd left, abandoning her instead of staying to make sure she had everything she needed.

A new pain slipped through him. She would think he didn't

care. That he didn't want to meet her newborns. The truth was, he desperately wanted to see the twin babes who put such a light in her eyes. Who turned her smile radiant.

I'm sorry, Telípe.

~

*L*ike a turtle peering from its shell, Chogan peeped through the entrance hole in his cave. Though his body still ached and his belly rumbled, he felt more alive than he had in days. In truth, he had no idea how long he'd been laid low with the sickness. He'd drunk all the water in his pouch, so the creek would be his first destination. His mouth ached like a stone seared by the scorching summer sun.

He climbed out of the cave, then pushed to standing, his legs wobbly like a new foal's. Though he may not have much more strength than a toddler, he was alive.

As he left the black rock area and padded through the woods to the creek at the base of the hill, he breathed in the fresh air. The stink of sweat and sickness hovered around him. Once he drank his fill, he could give himself a good dowsing.

He'd need to hunt soon, but he'd not brought his bow and quiver this time, only the knife that hung around his neck. A bit more rest through the afternoon might steady his aim, and then he could hunt for small game before the sun set. His belly growled at the thought of fresh cooked meat.

When he reached the trickle of water that could barely be called a creek, he knelt in a quick-flowing spot and ducked his mouth into the water to guzzle. The liquid flowed through him like the sweetest nectar, and he gulped over and over, finally quenching the parched surface of his mouth and throat. The cool liquid even eased the nausea in his belly.

At last, he raised up on hands and knees, heaving in fresh breaths of the life-giving air. Now, he felt truly alive.

After bending low for another long drink, he straightened and refilled his leather pouch with clearwater.

A twig snapped in front of him.

He froze, his eyes jerking forward to find the predator. That sound was sharp enough to be intentional. Most likely a warrior ready to make his presence known.

A pair of moccasins caught his gaze, and he lifted his chin to see the rest of the person. Every part of him tensed for action— either to leap forward to defend himself or spring back to stand and put himself on level ground with the intruder. For the moment, all weakness seemed to have fled, replaced by the blood pumping through him.

A glimpse of the stranger's face sent two thoughts crashing through him. A warrior yes, but this was no man.

And he'd seen her strength in battle before.

CHAPTER 6

*L*ike a wildcat studying her prey, the woman warrior eyed Chogan.

"Peace." He spoke the word in her language. As slowly as he could manage, he lifted himself to his feet, keeping his hands far away from his body so he didn't appear threatening. "I mean no harm."

He worked hard to hide the lingering exertion stealing his breath. Could she see his weakness? He wouldn't hurt this woman unless it came down to his life, and even then, he would only wound her enough to gain the upper hand. But he also didn't want her to think she could take advantage easily.

She wore a bow and quiver, as well as a knife and tomahawk. He'd seen her use that bow back when she and her band had come to free Telípe. The woman could send two arrows arcing to their target in the space of a breath.

For a long moment, she studied him. He returned the look, though her gaze said she'd like to pitch that knife into his heart. She certainly recognized him.

He couldn't blame her for wanting revenge against one of those who'd put her sister and the babes in such danger. If he had that journey to do over again, he would never have obeyed his father's command to go on the slave-capturing mission. On the other hand, he was glad he'd been there to help Telípe and the others who were taken.

Did this woman also remember how he'd helped her sister? How Telípe had stood between them to keep Meksem from killing him during the rescue?

At last, the words she ground out gave his answer. "For my sister's sake, I will not kill you now. But you will come with me and tell why you have come across the mountains again." She slid her gaze in a quick glance around them. "Where are the others?" She accompanied that last statement with the same question asked through signs.

Better he tell all now. If he was to have any chance with these people, even merely the chance to leave with his life, honesty would be crucial.

"I speak and understand your language. And there is no one with me. I've been sent away from my village and have come west toward the great ocean." Should he say anything about staying in this area to help Telípe before he moved on? Perhaps he better not offer that bit of news yet. This woman might slice him through if she thought he'd come to kidnap her sister again.

Her brow lowered the slightest bit, as though his answer didn't please her. She sent another gaze around, then drew her knife from its pouch and used the blade to motion in the direction of their village. "Walk."

He would have to obey. His strength might fail him if he tried to resist, especially with her knife already in her hand. And maybe it was best he finally stripped away the secrecy and presented himself to her people. This situation could go either way—they might kill him as soon as Meksem brought him. If their ways were anything like his own people's, it would be a long, torturous death.

Or they might give him the chance to prove himself. But

prove himself to be what? Friend? Or merely strong and valiant enough to fight bravely against a whole village of warriors?

If only he wasn't in this alone. The great spirit might have brought him here, but that being didn't step in to help, only used events to weigh a man's abilities.

At the moment, Chogan wasn't sure he could accomplish what was being set before him.

And what of Telípe? If he were burned to ashes or knifed to death in a gauntlet, he would never be able to help her as he so desired.

The thought of never seeing her again brought more pain in his chest than any other chaos coursing through his mind.

He marched in front of Meksem, following the route she directed. There were surely many ways back to her village, and it might not bode well for him to let on that he knew the path, at least the one that led to the edge of the trees where he could see the lodges.

Of course, Telípe might tell her people of the times she'd seen him. Just because she'd saved him once—and seemed to have kept his presence a secret—didn't mean she wouldn't be honest if asked, especially by those she loved.

~

*W*orry churned in Telípe's belly as she trudged back to the village. Why had Chogan never come? For three days now, she'd packed up the babes and taken her midday walk to the place they'd agreed to meet. Each day, more of her strength returned, so she'd climbed up the hill to the tree where he'd hidden those first two times. Today she'd even ventured farther.

Chogan never came. She'd been careful these last two days to make sure no one followed her, so that couldn't be the reason for his absence. Had he left the area, even though he'd said he would stay until his work was finished here?

She wasn't entirely sure what he considered his work to be, but he'd agreed to meet her and then never showed. Certainly, he wouldn't think his work complete, would he? Unless she really was of such little importance to him that he didn't count her in his plans.

That thought didn't ring true either. Their connection had hung thick between them these last few meetings. He wouldn't desert her unless something important required it.

Or unless he was *unable* to come.

The new thought twisted her middle, raising bile to her throat. Should she go search for him? Maybe he'd been injured while hunting. Or the wildcat...

If only she had a way of knowing. Meksem spoke of finding her new God's leading when Adam read in the pages of his book. The Bible, she called it.

If Telípe went to Adam and asked him to read—or maybe she could ask Susanna—would their God give her directions too? Or did she have to be a follower of His to receive His guiding? Was He really as all-knowing and powerful as her sister said?

As she neared the edge of the village, the twisting in her gut didn't subside, but this time it came from a different source. Soon she would need to leave the women's hut and return to the lodge of her brother. The grandmother was eager to help with the babes, and the extra hands would be nice. But the thought of going back to all that chaos pressed a burn in her belly. And Pisákas spent so much time there, escaping his watchful gaze would be so much harder.

The quiet of the women's lodge made it a haven. If only her brother would help her set up her own lodge. But if she asked, he would only tell her she should accept Pisákas. That the man had a perfectly good lodge in need of a woman's touch. A son in need of a mother.

The thought settled like spoiled meat in her belly. Not that she minded caring for the boy. But the man...she couldn't reconcile with joining herself to another man so soon, not one she barely knew or liked.

A call sounded at the far end of the village, nearest the trees. That was the same area where Meksem and her friends stayed. She strained to see what was happening there. The voice had sounded like one of the braves, maybe even Uyítpe, the chief. Had they caught the wildcat?

She turned her steps that direction and lengthened her stride. More people gathered as she approached, though everyone seemed to linger back, forming a large half circle around whatever caused the excitement. She wasn't tall enough to see over most of the forms, so she moved around to approach from the side.

Meksem's voice drifted to her, speaking with a man, maybe Uyítpe. But only a few words rose over the murmurs of the crowd. "He...found...said..."

She finally reached one end of the half circle and stepped around to see better.

Chogan's tall form came clear. A tiny cry escaped her, and she stepped forward before her mind caught up with her feet.

Meksem swung her attention away from the chief she'd been speaking with and pierced Telípe with her gaze.

What should she do? Meksem looked angry, though she covered it well with her warrior's glare.

And Chogan. He stood stiff and straight with no sign of injury that she could see. But something about him... There wasn't the easy strength that normally cloaked him. His skin seemed paler than usual. Was he...ill?

She took a step forward, then stopped herself again. She'd better deal with Meksem before speaking to Chogan.

Turning on her sister, she lifted her chin and summoned every bit of strength and certainty she could muster as she closed the distance between them. Better to keep their voices quiet so this didn't become a matter for the entire village. Although with so many people gathered, that possibility might not be avoided.

"What are you doing with him?" She addressed Meksem but included Uyítpe in her question. Since Meksem had already brought him into the circle, he would want to be included.

Meksem regarded her with an emotionless expression. "He is Blackfoot, our enemy. One of those who took you captive."

Telípe worked to school her face instead of giving Meksem the look she wanted to. She couldn't let herself come across as a young girl stamping her foot to get her way. She would only be heard if she showed wisdom and maturity. "He protected me and my unborn children. They may not be alive in my arms now if not for his kindness."

Meksem didn't blink. "He was hiding outside of our village, just as he and his brothers did when they took you and the others captive." She swung her attention to Uyítpe. "He said he was alone, but some of our warriors should search the black rock area to see if he lies."

Uyítpe turned and barked to four men standing nearby. Meksem used the distraction to refocus on Telípe, and her tone softened, changing from the stayed voice of a warrior to that of an older sister. "He speaks our language, Telípe. Why did he pretend not to know it before? We can't trust him." Her eyes dimmed with worry.

Telípe had to soothe the concern. Maybe if Meksem knew everything, she would not be so suspicious of him. Should Telípe tell her now that she'd already seen Chogan? That he'd explained to her why he didn't use their language before?

Uyítpe had turned back to them and studied her intently. Waiting for her to speak. Waiting to decide whether she should be heard and her words valued. This might be a better conversation with Meksem alone.

For now, she needed to get Chogan in a safe place.

She slipped a glance toward him, and the sight affirmed her decision. To an unfamiliar eye, he might look like any strong brave in the prime of his condition. But there was something about him, the tightness, the shift in his coloring, that showed he wasn't well.

She turned her focus back to Meksem and Uyítpe. "Hold him in the supply lodge. Let us get to know him and decide if he can be trusted. He showed nothing but kindness to me before, when it was in his power to treat me and the other captives harshly. In truth, the other braves with him scorned him for his actions, but he continued with honor and goodness. It would be wrong for us to treat him now with disrespect."

Meksem turned to Uyítpe. Perhaps she gave her opinion with her eyes, Telípe couldn't see for sure. But the man finally nodded. "Place him in the supply lodge. Have him bound and a guard assigned at all times. We will see what his intentions are, then decide."

"No." A new voice rose from the crowd as a man stepped forward. Pisákas.

Why did he always step in to meddle when he wasn't wanted. It wasn't as if she'd given him rights over her. Just because her brother wished a union between them didn't mean she'd agreed to it. Yet she couldn't refute him aloud in front of all these people, not without consequences.

The chief turned to Pisákas and waited for him to speak further.

Pisákas joined them with his chin raised—maybe in determination, but it struck her more as defiance. "He is Blackfoot. We can't allow him to stay in our village, even for one sleep." His tone held a vehemence that seemed too strong for this situation.

Then a memory slipped in. She'd lived in the Salish village

when Pisákas's wife had died, but hadn't she heard the woman succumbed to an illness some of their people had contracted in a Blackfoot camp? No wonder he felt strongly that a Blackfoot brave shouldn't be allowed in their village. Though that sickness was hardly the entire tribe's fault, simply hearing the Blackfoot name might bring him pain.

Still… She glanced at Chogan and couldn't miss the sheen of sweat across his brow. His eyes carried a dullness, nothing like their usual intensity. He needed care, and soon.

Preparing herself with a breath for courage, she addressed the chief. "What good would it do to send him away? I believe he is trustworthy, and if we hold him in the supply lodge, we can learn more about him." And nurse him through whatever ailed him. "He'll be kept separate from our people." She sent Pisákas a pacifying look. But a question niggled in her chest even as she spoke. Could Chogan's sickness possibly be the same thing that Pisákas's wife had died from? Surely not. That disease had created pox marks all over the invalid's face. Chogan showed no sign of that.

Pisákas's chin jutted even farther. "He shouldn't even be allowed in our village. Who knows what vile ailment he carries?"

Uyítpe straightened, a sign he'd made a decision on the matter. "We'll hold him in the supply lodge until we know more about him and his purpose here. That will be far enough away for our people to be safe."

Relief swept through Telípe as the chief stepped away, clearly marking the conversation as over. She didn't dare look at Pisákas, but she couldn't stop a glance toward Chogan as she clutched Kapskáps to her shoulder. He was watching her, and though he still held himself in the bearing of a warrior, his gaze had softened. His focus shifted from her face to the bundle at her shoulder. This was his first glimpse of her little ones, though she couldn't show them as she wanted to.

She would go to him though. Find out what was wrong with him and do everything in her power to bring him back to health. She had a purpose now, and to accomplish it, she no longer minded moving back to her brother's lodge. She would do whatever it took to help this man, who'd already impacted her in more ways than she was ready to admit.

CHAPTER 7

"*A*t last, you have brought more grandchildren to me." Ámtiz's grandmother lifted Éisnin near, the lines around her mouth wreathing in a smile. "This one has your nose and cheeks."

Telípe couldn't help but grin as she watched the sweet older woman interact with her little ones. Maybe Telípe shouldn't have dreaded moving back to this lodge. This grandmother really would be a great help, even though her age kept her from moving around much. Just the extra set of willing and capable hands to occupy the babes meant much.

While the grandmother continued to murmur over the girls, Telípe refocused her attention on the stew. She'd put everything into it she could think of to help Chogan. Meat to give strength to his body, bits of camas root that would help in many ways, including to gain the weight he'd lost.

The door flap rustled behind her, and Elan slipped in carrying a piece of buckskin gathered at its four corners to hold whatever lay inside.

She knelt beside Telípe and spread open the leather. "I

brought some roots that should help him. Winter cherry for strength and greenbrier to rid him of anything bad he might have eaten."

Telípe reached for one of the roots and begin to cut it into the stewpot. "Thank you." The words didn't begin to express how grateful she was for this woman. Elan had followed her back to the women's lodge after Meksem led Chogan away. It was as though Elan knew she planned to move and would need help.

Or maybe she simply realized Telípe *always* needed help. Caring for two needy babes proved so much harder than she'd ever imagined.

The moment she'd told Elan about the need to move back to her brother's lodge and prepare healing food for Chogan, the woman set to work without questions. Not even how she knew Chogan was sick.

Before the soup was ready, Kapskáps began fussing to be fed. Éisnin would be hungry soon too, and it was better to get the nursing out of the way before she went to see Chogan. Should she bring the babes with her this time? She'd need help to carry them and the food both. Perhaps it would be best for her to visit him alone first. Maybe what he had was catching. The last thing she wanted to do was put the babes in danger. Their tiny bodies seemed too delicate to ward off sickness.

While she nursed the children, the grandmother laid down to rest and Elan tended the stew. Her brother's wife had taken their two energetic younger brothers to fish in the river. As much as Telípe enjoyed their company, especially individually when they were a little quieter, their absence cast a peacefulness over the lodge she couldn't help but savor.

The babes dozed as each finished nursing, so she swaddled them tight and laid them on their mat.

When she rejoined Elan by the fire, the woman was

spooning out a helping of soup. "I'll stay here and help if the little ones wake."

She took the bowl from Elan. "Thank you."

The woman met Telípe's gaze with a smile. "I'm sorry I wasn't there to meet Chogan the first time, but I heard about what he did for you. No matter what else he does or doesn't do, I'm thankful for his kindness then."

A knot of emotion rose up into her throat, clogging so she had to swallow to get words past it. "He's a good man. One of the best I've known."

Maybe she showed too much of her heart in those words, but Elan's smile turned sweeter. "Take this to him, then, and help him recover from whatever ails him."

With a nod, Telípe slipped from the lodge before she lost her chance.

The supply hut where they'd taken Chogan was at the far corner of the village, out of the way of the usual comings and goings as the people went about their work.

Hopefully Chogan's presence would be forgotten by most. Then, when the leaders were convinced he didn't intend a threat, he could begin to ease himself into the life of this place.

Would he consider staying? If he'd been cast out of his own town, maybe he would want to start a new life here.

She was fooling herself, though, to harbor any of these thoughts. The fact that the chief had agreed to hold him captive instead of killing him outright was surprising enough. The chance that Chogan might become one of them—and the chance of him even *wanting* that—were almost too small to consider.

When she reached the storage lodge, the posted guard stepped from inside the teepee. Tékes had been given this first watch, and she summoned a serene smile for him. "I brought food for the prisoner." She should have brought something for Tékes as well. Why hadn't she thought of that?

Of course, his wife was one of the best cooks in the village. Nothing Telípe made would compare. But maybe...

She well remembered how much he'd looked up to her eldest brother when they were little more than lads. Perhaps this was a gift she could offer. "Síkem mentioned he's been planning to ask you to go on a hunt with him. The elk have been seen nearby, and he wants to stock up before the cool weather comes." Her brother *had* mentioned he planned to set out on an elk hunt soon. Surely he wouldn't mind taking this old friend along.

A spark brightened the man's eyes.

She stepped past him into the lodge. Tékes entered behind her but stayed back near the door to allow her room to move in the small circle where the supplies had been pushed back for Chogan to sit.

His eyes locked on her the moment she stepped into the lodge. He must've heard her voice from outside.

She met his gaze as she dropped to her knees before him. She'd planned to search his face for a sign of what might be wrong, but she couldn't look away from the intensity of his eyes. His gaze held a hunger and drew her in as though she could meet his need.

"Chogan." His name slipped out in a whisper.

His mouth parted, but he said nothing.

She finally tore her focus from his, dropping her gaze to the bowl in her hands. She lifted the stew as she glanced back up at him. "I brought you soup." This time she didn't let her eyes meet his but scanned his face and down to his shoulders. He *had* lost weight, and a sheen of sweat glistened over his skin. Perhaps others might think he was simply warm from the lack of air flowing inside this lodge, but the scent of sickness lingered around him.

Her heart ached with whatever he'd suffered. "What's wrong?"

The lines at the corners of his eyes gathered, drawing her focus back to them. "Nothing now." His gaze caressed her face as his hands might've done if they weren't tied behind his back.

Heat flamed up her neck at the thought. She shouldn't feel that way about this man, but she couldn't seem to stop it.

She forced her mind to think, not to fall into the pools of his eyes and linger there. He'd said *nothing now*. Did he mean he'd been sick and was recovered? Her heart wanted it to mean her presence healed him, but that couldn't be the case.

Again, she forced her focus down to the bowl. With his hands tied, she could either feed him herself or ask the guard to free him. She doubted the latter would be allowed. And she longed to do the former.

She'd seen Meksem's white friends use a spoon, but she didn't have one. She shifted closer and lifted the bowl to Chogan's lips. His eyes moved from her face to the liquid as she tipped the container up to pour the soup in his mouth.

He gulped, the Adam's apple at his throat dipping, drawing her focus to the strong column of his neck. She lifted her gaze to his jaw, chiseled from stone by an expert craftsman. Every nuance, every feature, perfectly formed.

After four gulps, his gaze flicked up to her face, and he drew back. She lowered the bowl and glanced inside. He'd eaten about half, but he should let that settle before taking more.

Steeling herself against the power of his eyes, she looked up at him again. "You've been sick?"

He offered a single nod, and pain entered his gaze. He lowered his voice so the guard wouldn't hear. "I'm sorry I wasn't there to see the little ones."

She shrugged. She couldn't let him see how much she'd worried. She wasn't ready to reveal that much. "I didn't know if you'd left or if something happened."

Lines furrowed his brow as he studied her. "I told you I would not leave." His gaze slipped away. "It was the fever. I don't know how long. The first time I left my camp was when your sister found me."

A new surge of worry pressed through her. Had he been lying feverish and unaware all that time? She lifted her fingers to his brow to feel for heat. Maybe she shouldn't have, the way his gaze jerked to her face when she touched him. Even the guard behind her shifted enough for his buckskins to rustle.

But the heat emanating from Chogan's brow proved what the sweat had hinted at before. "You're still ill. You should be lying down." She glanced around the area where he sat. Nothing had been brought for him. He sat in the dirt beside the cold ashes of a long-ago fire, but no wood was laid for a new blaze. No furs to sleep on. "I'll bring blankets for you." She glanced back at him and lifted the bowl. "Can you finish this?"

He eyed the stew and seemed to gather himself before nodding. He likely wondered when, or if, he would be offered food again. But if he could keep this down, it would help him. Especially if he hadn't eaten much in days.

She lifted the bowl again and shifted sideways to be at a better angle to hold the dish. The position moved her closer to him, but she didn't let herself focus on his nearness.

When he finished the last swallow, she set the bowl aside. "Is there anything else you need?"

His hesitation made her hone in on his face. At last, he said, "Water."

Of course. She should've thought to bring something to drink.

Again, sorrow slipped into his gaze as he spoke. "I want to meet your daughters, but I don't want them to take on this illness. Nor you."

She worked for a smile to relieve his worries. "I'll be careful. And there will be time with them later."

He nodded, and she rose to go. Purpose surged through her

as she stopped to tell the guard she'd return soon with bedding and water. Finally, she had something she could do to make a difference, a mission only she could fulfill.

CHAPTER 8

*E*ven if Chogan's hands and feet weren't bound as he lay atop the furs Telípe had brought the day before, he wasn't sure he would've had enough strength to stand. The hike to the village had drained the last of his meager energy, and after Telípe had brought this soft bedding, sleep had overtaken him. He'd not awakened once through the night. When he did finally return to awareness, his guard had changed.

Telípe's sister, Meksem, now stood watchful, her attention split between eyeing him and peering through the opening to see any who approached. This lodge was built like those of his people, with skins stretched on poles and the hole for the door draped with a hanging fur. Thankfully, they kept that pelt tied back, probably for easy access, but it also allowed a bit of air inside. Even so, with the supplies stacked high around him, the place felt stuffy and dim.

Another woman had brought him food that morning, more of the same fare Telípe fed him the day before. This one said her name was Elan and that she was a friend of Telípe. She had a gentle way about her that soothed, and with the food, more water to ease his parched insides, and so much sleep, he finally felt more like himself.

If only he could get up and move around. But Meksem had commanded him to sit or lie on the fur unless ordered otherwise. He had to prove himself trustworthy, and that began with obedience.

Meksem hadn't questioned him yet. No one had. Which was strange. How could they decide about him if they never took time to inquire?

When she stiffened and stepped outside, he worked himself upright. Had Telípe come to check on him?

The low hum of a male voice sounded before a tall brave slipped through the opening, Meksem entering behind him.

Not Telípe. Disappointment sank in his stomach like a stone.

Something about the man seemed familiar, and when he came near enough for Chogan see his face clearly, realization swept through him. He was one of those who'd come to rescue Telípe. Chogan hadn't heard what tribe the man was from, but from the questions the others had asked him, Chogan had the feeling he was either Blackfoot or had lived with that tribe.

The man came near and lowered himself to sit opposite Chogan. "Oki."

Chogan took in the Blackfoot greeting with a nod. The man spoke as though that was his mother tongue. At least with that word. Chogan responded in the same language. "You are Blackfoot?"

The man nodded. "From a Peigan village along the river the white men call Marias."

That made more sense. Of the three groups the Blackfoot had split into, the Peigan tended to be more peaceful. Far less warlike than the Bloods, his own band. His people scoffed at the Peigan's weak-minded ways.

He'd given thought to finding a Peigan village after his father sent him away.

But he'd wanted to leave the Blackfoot name behind completely. Something about the west had called to him. He'd thought that pursuit had been the great spirit's guiding. Did he still believe that?

The brave didn't give him time to ponder but changed his language to that of the village around them. "I am called Beaver Tail. You understand the Nimiipuu tongue?"

Chogan nodded. "I do."

"Good. We will speak that language so Meksem can hear your words too."

Again he nodded. How had this Blackfoot man been accepted into the village, trusted enough that he would be allowed—even chosen—as the one to question a potential threat? Maybe the fact that Beaver Tail was Blackfoot made the others think he would see past any front Chogan tried to present. Yet, that proved even more that the man was trusted by these Nimiipuu people.

Beaver Tail didn't waste time on casual words. "You said you were sent away from your people. Why?"

He studied the man. To truly answer that question, he would have to start farther back. Hopefully, he wouldn't tell so much that these people would also disdain him. "My father is chief in that town. I am the third son, the last of my mother's living children. My brothers are great warriors with long strings of scalps and many horses they've stolen in their campaigns.

"From my youngest days, I didn't like the wargames we were taught to play. I could tell this displeased my father, and my brothers teased me for my weakness. But I've never had the desire to cause pain without reason.

"I have always tried to show my father the respect of his position and do his bidding. When he sent me on the hunts to bring in food for our people, I learned quickly. I brought in many buffalo and deer—more than my part. But when he sent me with the war parties to take scalps and bring back captives, my belly soured. I have no need to hang hair on a string. And I would sooner tend my own skins than steal a man's daughter to work them for me. I've seen my own mother's grief when my sister died. I would not bring that on someone else."

Now to answer the specific question the man had asked. "My peaceful actions embarrassed my father too many times. Last winter, he commanded me to accompany the braves through the mountains to take captives and prove myself worthy of his name. I went along. In my heart"—he pressed a fist to his chest —"I wanted to honor him. But the same heart takes no pleasure in bringing pain to others unjustly. As I watched the captives, I knew what I must do. And when I heard your sister"—he glanced at Meksem—"speak of being with child, I knew if she lost the babe, its death would be on my head." That familiar pain pressed in his chest, turning his gut. "So I did everything I could to protect her. To protect them all."

He was glad he'd done it, too, no matter how the flash of disappointment in his father's eyes had seared him. The anger that had taken over his expression was far easier to face. That anger had always riled Chogan's own, and he'd fought to hold his tongue as the man lashed into him with his words.

"And then?" Beaver Tail's prodding brought him back to the present.

"When I brought back the remnants of our group, injured and angry, my father laid the outcome to my account. If I hadn't been weak toward the captives, if I had fought like a man when their kinsman caught up with us, my people would have been valiant. Their mothers would not be childless. He said that he also lost a son on that hunt. I no longer lived in his eyes. He sent me away without my horse or gun."

As silence settled over them, Beaver Tail studied him, his dark eyes piercing. "Why did you not settle with others of the Blackfoot? The Peigan would have honored your wish to live peaceably."

Perhaps. He hadn't been certain. "I considered that, but I prayed that the great spirit would show me the path I should take. He led me in the direction of the setting sun. I thought to follow these rivers all the way to the great water I've heard of."

Beaver Tail's brows rose. "You have not reached the ocean yet."

Heat slid up Chogan's neck. That must be the man's way of asking why he'd stopped short of that goal. Now was the time where he needed to speak of Telípe. Would it put her in trouble? Probably.

Yet, she was a grown woman with children of her own, not a maiden still under the care of her parents. But consorting with the enemy—that was likely an action that would bring the censure of the entire village down on her.

He studied Beaver Tail. Then flicked a glance at Meksem. She wouldn't wish her sister in trouble. He'd seen the affection between the two of them, the way Meksem protected Telípe. If anything he said would bring harm to Telípe, Meksem would control who learned of it.

Surely she would.

But what of the Blackfoot man? Again he studied Beaver Tail. There seemed a measure of respect between these two. Maybe even friendship. Could he trust this man? Beaver Tail, better than anyone else here, would know whether news of Telípe hiding Chogan's presence would hurt her. Beaver may have experienced firsthand any anger these people held toward the Blackfoot. Chogan would have to trust these two.

Beaver Tail didn't prod him to continue this time. Maybe he realized Chogan wasn't lost in thought but waring within himself. This might be a crucible, a test whether he would speak the truth or not.

That firmed his decision. "I knew I was nearing the western edge of the mountains, but I intentionally chose a path south of the village where I thought Telípe lived, the place we'd taken her from before." That fact was important for them to understand. He'd not sought out a woman he knew to be married, no matter how much his heart had been pulled toward her.

Beaver Tail's gaze never wavered, just watched him with his deep intensity.

"I was surprised when I met her in the woods. She was picking berries and large with child." He held his hand out in front of his belly to show just how big. "When I spoke with her and she told of the reason she came to this place, my heart was filled with knowing." Again he pressed a fist to his chest. "For this reason, the great spirit led me to this place. To help this woman who helped me before." Meksem would remember well how Telípe had stood in front of Chogan, protecting him when Meksem wanted to run a blade through during the battle to free the captives.

Meksem shifted from where she crouched behind Beaver Tail. Though her expression hadn't changed, something in her bearing rose up, that protectiveness he'd seen from her before when she thought he was a threat to her sister.

Did she still think he would do something to hurt Telípe? Or was it merely the fact he was Blackfoot and she didn't trust his people?

At least he could prove himself on the first count. "I wasn't sure what the great spirit wished me to help her with, but I gave her food from my hunting."

"You saw her more than once?" Meksem's voice pulled tight as she bit the words.

He nodded. "Twice before the babes were born. Once more after. I warned her of the wildcats I'd heard fighting. Gave her meat from the smaller male I hunted. I wanted to help her any way I could. I had no other reason to see her." That wasn't entirely true. But he'd *wanted* that to be his motive. "But then the sickness struck me with fever for several sleeps. I do not know how many. My strength was finally coming back to me the same day you found me by the river." He addressed that last bit to Meksem.

The rest they knew. He worked to keep from fidgeting as he waited. The two shared a glance, but he couldn't read their thoughts in the look. They must know each other well to have communicated anything at all.

At last, Beaver Tail turned back to him and studied him a moment longer before speaking. "I will tell these people what you have said. They will decide what is to be done with you."

The man rose, Meksem with him. Didn't they have questions? Surely his story hadn't been so thorough they had nothing more to ask.

As Beaver Tail stepped out of the lodge, Meksem took up her previous position by the entrance. But as she glanced outside, her face formed a frown. She followed him out.

Another voice sounded outside, one deliciously familiar. The voice that always soothed his tension. Telípe spoke in low tones, and her sister responded in the same quiet voice, though there was nothing gentle in her sound.

Had Telípe just approached? Or had she been standing outside listening? He'd told her some of his story before, though not the details of his childhood. He would gladly tell her even more if she asked.

Yet something about the thought of her knowing so much about him—so many personal details… Well, the idea seemed intimate.

Telípe's voice rose loud enough for him to hear. "He has to eat, Meksem. He's recovering from sickness."

Meksem's voice stayed too low to decipher words. The elder sister clearly didn't trust him yet.

"Meksem." Telípe's voice held a warning he'd only heard from her one other time, the time she'd stood between him and her sister's blade.

Again, Meksem's voice hummed through the door flap, too low to make out.

"Then untie his hands so he can feed himself." Telípe's tread sounded outside before she appeared in the opening and stepped in carrying a bowl and a bark plate.

She sent him a smile that warmed his insides like the sun's rays. But she didn't pause to greet him. Just dropped to her knees on the fur in front of him and laid the food between them.

"Wait." Agitation edged Meksem's voice as she marched toward him and stepped around to his back. Her knife blade sliced the cord around his wrists, and pain shot through his arms as he eased them apart. He'd been in that position a full day, and his limbs had grown numb. Now, tiny stings peppered his skin as he slid his hands around to his lap.

Meksem moved back to crouch in front of him and, without a word, gathered his wrists and retied them. At least with them in front, he could feed himself. She'd sliced the lacing in such a way that she had plenty of cord to fasten a tight knot. When she finished, she checked the binding, then rose to her feet.

Telípe sent her sister a sideways look that seemed to hold part amusement and part frustration. He couldn't blame Meksem for her protectiveness. In truth, he was thankful for it. Thankful Telípe had this strong warrior to watch out for her. If only he could prove to the woman he would do no harm, only good.

Telípe shifted her gaze to him with an apologetic smile, and he did his best with his eyes to tell her not to worry about her sister.

Then he shifted his focus to the food. As he took in the savory aroma of stew and camas cake, his belly grumbled. He'd already eaten once that day when Elan came, but his body seemed desperate to make up for what he'd lost during the sickness.

Cupping the bowl with both hands, he lifted it to his mouth. He sent a glance to Telípe and used his eyes to offer a smile of thanks as he swallowed the first bite. He'd never tasted Nimi-ipuu food before yesterday. These people seemed to live more heavily on camas root and salmon than his people did, but the food's flavor wove through him in a pleasing way.

Telípe's eyes scanned him while he ate, as though searching for something. At last, her words told him what she sought. "You are better?"

He nodded. "Good food, soft furs. Much better." He didn't dare say more with the weight of her sister's glare on them both.

Telípe must have felt it too, for she smiled, then rose. "One of us will bring food when the sun sets." She sent a glance to her sister as she spoke, and Meksem nodded.

Then Telípe turned back to him, and her smile slid through him, strengthening every part it touched.

He managed a simple reply. "Thank you." He could only hope she read the depth of his feelings in his eyes.

As she nodded, then turned to leave, he fought with himself not to watch her go.

He had a feeling the woman left standing guard would play a significant role in whether he lived or died. Better he control his longings than raise her ire.

CHAPTER 9

"*Y*ou met him in secret, Telípe? Why? Why would you do this thing?"

Telípe cringed as her sister released the force of her frustration, now that they were finally away from the village and listening ears. She offered Meksem a repentant smile. "I'm sorry you're angry."

Meksem threw a hand up between them. "You're right. You're sorry I'm angry, but you're not sorry to have met with this man—this stranger, this enemy warrior who kidnapped you. And you met him *in secret*, when no one knew the danger you were in. No one was there to protect you should your belief in him be wrong."

No matter how many times Telípe reminded herself Meksem's frustration came from care for her, she couldn't help the way her sister's words raised her own annoyance. "The first time I saw him in the woods, I didn't know I'd be meeting him. He did me no harm, and I saw clearly that he wouldn't hurt me. He had countless opportunities to take advantage during the kidnapping, and he was nothing but kind. Even to his own loss, he's been generous and honorable."

Dare she say what she really wanted to? Yes. "In fact, I trust him more than I do some of the braves from our own village."

Meksem's mouth pinched. She must realize Telípe meant Pisákas. Her sister raised her gaze to the distant horizon. "I've remained silent regarding Pisákas, because I didn't want to pressure you into a marriage you don't wish for. But I think your life would be easier if you marry a Nimiipuu brave, not one our people distrust."

Telípe swallowed her first retort, then worked for a calmer way to respond. "Do you speak from experience? You would have rather taken the easy path to marry a Nimiipuu than Adam?"

Meksem's gaze jerked to her face, eyes sparking. "You know I didn't mean that."

"But it's the same thing." Surely Meksem saw that. In Telípe's arms, Kapskáps squirmed in her sleep. Telípe bobbed a little and tightened her hold on the bundle to soothe the child as she lowered her voice for Meksem. "I simply want you to give him a fair chance. Hear his words and judge the merit of his actions on their own. Don't let your protectiveness for me sway your judgment."

Meksem met her gaze, and her eyes softened. They'd not had such a hard conversation before, but these things had to be said. Her sister was wise, and she would realize the truth in Telípe's words, whether she wanted to or not.

At last, Meksem offered a sad smile. "Adam says the same thing."

Telípe's grin slipped out in full. "You married a wise man."

Meksem nodded even as she shifted her focus forward. Ahead of them, their brother's wife had brought the boys to the river again. This seemed to be a place she came often with them. A kindness to her grandmother, no doubt.

This sweet woman had been good for their family. Patient with the boys—at least more so than many would be. Marriage to her had helped their elder brother grow up quickly. Or maybe the death of their parents had done that.

In the cradleboard on Meksem's back, Éisnin began to stretch too. Telípe dropped back to see her youngest and tucked her finger around the chubby hand. The babe blinked at her and offered that half smile that would win anyone's heart.

Then she moved back up to Meksem's side again. Two sisters carrying two sisters, it felt right, sharing her daughters with Meksem. She glanced sideways at her. "Any thoughts of having your own wee one soon?"

She'd never seen Meksem blush, not even when the boys teased her as a child. Back then, she'd merely clamped her jaw and worked harder to best them. But this was surely a blush creeping up to darken her already tanned cheeks. She shook her head. "Not really."

By that reaction, *not really* probably meant not anything she was ready to speak of. Telípe's grin was impossible to hold inside.

They reached the river's edge and stopped beside Ámtiz, their sister-in-law, who was kneeling over a deer skin, working it with a rock to soften the hide. She rose to sit on her heels and offered a greeting. "You're much recovered, I see." Her gaze studied Telípe as though to make sure her words were true.

Telípe nodded. "The babes and I both needed time away from camp." She'd not gone on her walk the day before. Instead, she'd taken food to Chogan and overheard his conversation with Beaver Tail and Meksem. This was the first chance she'd had to get Meksem away to talk about things.

A shout from the boys pulled their focus toward the river, where the lads were playing upstream. The youngest jumped on the other to dunk him under, which started a wrestling match.

Ámtiz sighed. "I brought them here to fish, but they like this better. Síkem says they should be learning how to provide for the family as men do." Her voice turned wistful. "They take such pleasure in swimming, it's hard to make them do something I know they dislike. Especially in the heat of the day."

The piercing sun did seem hotter this day than before. Telípe sank to the grass and laid Kapskáps in front of her, spreading out the blanket to give the babe some air.

Meksem sat too and pulled off the cradleboard. Her fingers worked the straps easily as she pulled Éisnin out.

Her sister-in-law reached for Kapskáps and held her up. "Look at how much she's grown." She drew the baby close and cooed to her.

Kapskáps pursed her bow-shaped lips and responded with a babble of her own.

Warmth washed through Telípe. That was the first time her eldest daughter had made such a noise. Éisnin had nearly come out of the womb chattering, but this was a new milestone for Kapskáps.

As her sisters interacted with the babes on either side of her, Telípe let her eyes close under the warmth of the summer sun. How strange to be sitting here with these two married women, her babes fully loved by them. The sensation felt off, like someplace she'd visited in a dream. But when she went there in reality, nothing was quite as in her imaginings.

A husband. She was the only one of these matrons who no longer had a man to stand beside her.

The image that slipped in was no longer Heinmot, and certainly not Pisákas, but Chogan. Did that make her terrible? Ungrateful for all Heinmot had done for her? She *was* grateful. He'd been a kind husband when so many who entered an arranged marriage suffered under the hand of a cruel master.

But the feelings stirring within her for Chogan were not like anything she'd ever experienced.

A scream pierced her thoughts.

She jerked her eyes open, scanning the river, jerking her focus toward the boys splashing.

Another gut-wrenching cry came from their direction. She leapt to her feet, but Meksem was already two steps ahead. The boys thrashed in the water. What could have happened to them? If they were moving, it couldn't be that one had hit his head on a rock. The river was too shallow there for one to be drowning.

Meksem leapt up the bank to reach a place even with the boys. Ámtiz helped Telípe settle the babes where they would be safe in the grass, then they both ran in Meksem's wake. As they neared, the danger came clear.

The wildcat.

Telípe's heart surged into her throat as the animal clung to the back of her middle brother, Gezíu. The lad spun in the water, falling backward to dunk the creature in the river. Zílmii, the baby of the family, stood a few steps back, his screams turned to fearful cries.

Meksem stood on the edge of the bank peering intently into the water. Searching for her mark before she plunged in.

In the next breath, Gezíu roared up from the water, the giant cat still clutching his back. The boy's howls filled the air.

Meksem charged into the river, knife raised. She pushed through the waist deep current as she worked frantically to reach them.

Not Gezíu. Telípe couldn't breathe as the scene unfolded. She had no weapon with her. No way to help.

The boy plunged backward into the water again, disappearing under the murky surface. He must be trying to dislodge the creature, and surely water would work as well as anything.

Meksem reached them, but she could do nothing until they rose without risking plunging her blade into their brother instead of the beast.

She grabbed for the boy's arm and found purchase, pulling him up while raising the knife to strike as soon as she had a clear view of the animal.

The moment the boy's head cleared the surface, his howls

grew even louder. Blood clouded the water, making it even harder to see through the murkiness.

Telípe's pulse pounded and she charged into the river. As soon as Meksem killed the animal, she would need help with Gezíu.

At last, Meksem must have found a clear angle to the cat. She struck hard, a war cry echoing from deep inside her.

The boy's wails still filled the air, and as Telípe fought the current, she lost sight of what was happening ahead.

When she finally reached them, Meksem was rising up from the water, pulling their brother along with her. On the far bank, the wildcat sprang from one rock to another, fleeing the carnage.

His howls had turned to sobs, and bloody water ran from him in sheets. The flesh on his shoulders hung in shreds. Pain twisted his face, pressing hard on Telípe's chest.

Telípe grabbed one of his arms in a place that didn't look injured, and Meksem adjusted her hold on his other side. Together, they trudged toward the bank. Their littlest brother scurried ahead of them, and Ámtiz stood waiting for him with open arms.

The youngest boy ran to her, and she embraced him like the mother figure she'd become since their own mother's passing.

As Telípe and Meksem helped Gezíu up on the bank, his sobs quieted to heart-wrenching heaves. Telípe sent a glance toward her babes, nestled safely on the grass. She needed to help Meksem take the lad home, but she couldn't leave her daughters.

"Go." Ámtiz waved her forward, one arm still around the younger boy's shoulders. "I'll put Éisnin back in the cradleboard and bring them both. Help him."

Telípe searched the woman's urgent gaze. Yes, Ámtiz would take care with the children. She nodded and focused her attention on her brother as they limped toward the village.

~

*V*oices clamored somewhere in the village, and Chogan's guard leapt to his feet and stepped outside the lodge. Chogan strained to hear what was happening. Did he dare stand and move toward the opening so he could see more than the gray skins of the lodge next door?

No. He couldn't give them any thought that he might use this distraction to escape. Instead, he strained his ears and watched his guard for signs of what was happening.

The voices grew louder and closer. He could finally pick out a few words. "Arms...boy...cat."

His body tensed. Had someone found the wildcat? Had the creature hurt one of the villagers? A boy?

Fear coursed through him. He'd searched for that creature for days, but he'd had to hang back when the Nimiipuu braves began trailing him too. He'd finally been halted from his search completely by the sickness. If only he'd pressed harder when he had the chance.

If someone had been hurt by the animal...especially a child. Every part of him wanted to stand and sprint toward the gathered crowd to find out what had happened. If the creature still lived, he yearned to hunt it down now in earnest and stop the beast from injuring anyone else.

At last, the guard stepped back in, standing by the entrance where he could see outside and down the row.

"What is it? What's happened?" Chogan fisted his hands to keep from springing up.

"That wildcat attacked a boy." The man stood like a wildcat himself, coiled to spring outside at the first sign of more news.

"Who? Which boy? Is he hurt badly?" He likely wouldn't know the person, but he desperately wanted to know if he was one of Telípe's family. He hated the thought of anyone injured, but something inside him had to find out how much it affected Telípe.

The man sent him a quick glance. "Síkem's brother." Then he returned to staring anxiously toward the voices. "The glimpse I saw showed him bloody, but he was walking between his sisters."

He had no idea who Síkem was, but *between his sisters*. That could be Telípe and Meksem.

Another stir of commotion rang outside, this time the deeper sound of men's voices filling the air. The guard froze to listen, then with a final glance back at Chogan, he darted out the door.

Every part of him itched to follow. Could he at least stand and poke his head out to see what was happening? It sounded as though all the braves were being summoned.

Before he had to decide, another man appeared in the doorway, then stepped inside. Uyítpe, the chief. The man who'd first assigned Chogan to be guarded here instead of being killed when Meksem brought him into the village.

Behind the man, Beaver Tail approached, standing just outside the lodge. He watched Chogan but seemed to be standing back in deference to the first man. As though waiting his turn. Or maybe as backup in case he was needed. Maybe as interpreter? Chogan's Nimiiputimpt was decent enough Beaver shouldn't be needed in that role.

Chogan shifted his focus to Uyítpe as the man towered in front of him. "We will let you go free to prove your words. We ask only that, if you stay in this area, you will become a guest of our people. You will not camp in the rocks. If you wish to continue west, you may leave."

Relief washed through him, along with a bit of shock. He wasn't naïve enough to believe they offered him a place to stay out of kindness or honor. They wanted to keep an eye on him. But he didn't mind that a bit.

Uyítpe dropped to his haunches in front of Chogan and used his knife to slice through the bindings at his wrists and ankles.

Chogan didn't leap to his feet, but leveled his gaze on the man. "I will go with your men to hunt the wildcat. I was searching for him before. If I had tracked better then, the boy would not be injured now."

Uyítpe eyed him, maybe weighing the wisdom of allowing it. Staying motionless took every bit of control Chogan possessed. But the effort paid off when Uyítpe nodded, then rose and stepped back.

He glanced over his shoulder at Beaver Tail, then turned back to Chogan. "You are to stay with this man as his guest. You may go with him when he hunts."

Chogan looked past the chief to meet the Blackfoot brave's gaze. Did his eyes deceive him, or did Beaver Tail's expression contain the hint of a grin?

Maybe being this man's *guest* would be a gift. If Beaver could teach him how to win the favor of these people, Chogan would be more than grateful. And something about the man made him think that maybe—if Chogan didn't do something to ruin his chance—Beaver Tail might become a friend.

The thought called to him more than he should allow.

CHAPTER 10

*T*elípe smeared the last of the witch hazel poultice on her brother's back, then turned to rinse her hands in the bowl of water someone had brought to pour over the wounds. The grandmother sat with the boy's head in her lap, soothing him in the way only a grandmother could as she brushed her fingers through his hair.

The lad's tears had finally ebbed, his eyes drifting shut. Sleeping would be a challenge through the pain of his injuries, but if he could find rest, he should take it.

When Telípe glanced at the grandmother, the older woman nodded, her eyes saying they'd done everything they could for now. Gezíu had lost much blood, and wildcat scratches were known to blister and ooze, sometimes taking lives from fever many sleeps after the attack.

She would come back to check on him, but for now, she needed to see about the twins. Colette and Susanna had taken them to the lodge the women shared with their husbands and friends so the babes wouldn't be in the way while Telípe helped care for Gezíu's wounds. But the little ones would likely be hungry by now.

As she stepped out of her family's lodge, a flurry of activity swirled in the camp. The braves must be readying to hunt the cat. Surely they would find the creature this time. How could a single animal—savvy wildcat though it be—elude an entire village of seasoned warriors?

Éisnin's sweet voice sounded from inside the Lodge as Telípe approached. "Ga, ga." The babe could already manage something like a babble, and she made the sounds anytime she was pleased.

Adult voices murmured along with the babe's, the rumble of men among them. Some of the white men must be readying for the hunt.

The door flap was tied back to allow the breeze and sunlight through, and she poked her head inside before stepping in. The sight there was so different from what she'd expected, she blinked to make sure she wasn't seeing things.

Chogan. He knelt on the ground and held Éisnin in front of him. His large hands cupped the babe's head, and her body rested along the length of his forearms. The two studied each other as though fascinated, each with the other. Telípe's heart ached with the pleasure the sight brought.

Maybe Chogan felt her gaze, for he glanced her direction. The lines at the corners of his eyes crinkled, but the smile held a hint of sadness.

She stepped into the lodge, and the edge of her gaze cataloged Elan holding Kapskáps. But her focus shifted back to Chogan. When had he been allowed to leave his guard? Had he been released fully?

She moved to his side, then lowered to her knees. Her mouth formed a smile, though her throat had tightened so much her breaths could barely squeeze through. The questions no longer seemed important, not as she watched this strong man treasure her child like the greatest gift.

"You've met them." She tore her gaze from the man to take in her second born. Éisnin had shifted her focus from Chogan to Telípe, her mouth opening in that way she did as a first sign of hunger.

But Telípe didn't want to take the baby yet. She wanted to linger here with this man and revel in the joy of introducing him to her little ones.

"She is happy, this one." His voice rumbled with pleasure. Then he turned to look at Kapskáps in Elan's arms. "And this one, she is determined."

A laugh slipped through her, pitched higher than her usual tone. "You know them well already."

Elan lifted Kapskáps toward Telípe with raised brows, and Telípe took the babe. She laid her across her legs in the same position Chogan held Éisnin, but Kapskáps strained her tiny body upward as though trying to reach her mother. She was probably hungry, too, but to hold her off awhile longer, Telípe lifted the babe to rest against her shoulder.

Chogan's eyes followed the little one, lingering on the tiny face at Telípe's shoulder. The gentleness in his gaze, the tenderness softening his expression, wove through her like a soothing balm. What man could be such a strong warrior and yet so tender with these babes?

That thought brought back her earlier questions, and though she'd like to simply enjoy watching him, she needed answers. "They let you go free?"

He lifted his gaze from Kapskáps to Telípe's face. "I am to be a guest in the camp while I stay in this area. If I leave, I am to leave the entire territory." A smile touched his eyes again, but this time it contained no sadness. "They wish to keep watch on me, but I don't mind. Beaver Tail has taken me into this lodge and is allowing me to go with him on the hunt for the wildcat."

A pang of apprehension pressed through her. "You're going out? When?"

He glanced toward the door. "All of the able men in the

village are going. Beaver Tail has gone to find my weapons the men brought from my camp, then we'll be off. We'll form small groups and travel in all directions." His voice hardened. "We will catch this enemy before it can hurt another."

She should be relieved he was going with Beaver Tail and other braves, but fear gripped her throat and nearly cut off her breath. The wounds on her brother's back and shoulders had been impossibly deep. Unspeakably painful.

The animal had been forced to flee without its prey. Perhaps it was also wounded. It would be angry—and even more daring from hunger and pain.

As though he followed the line of her thoughts, Chogan's brows tented over worried eyes. "How is your brother? He'll recover?"

She swallowed to speak past the lump in her throat. "I hope so. If the wounds don't fester. He's in much pain though."

Chogan's gaze caressed her face with a gentle touch, but the sadness in his eyes brought a burn to her own. "I'm sorry, Telípe."

Kapskáps released a complaint. Not quite a cry but a noise loud enough to express her frustration that her mother hadn't recognized her more subtle hunger cues. If Telípe didn't take her now and give her the meal she wanted, earnest cries would come soon.

"I need to take them." She kept her focus on Éisnin's face, not glancing at Chogan. Yet still, heat crept up to her ears. Would he guess why she needed to take them? A mother feeding her babes was the most natural thing, yet speaking of it with this man...

Before Chogan could answer, before she could even gauge whether he understood what the babes needed, a man appeared in the doorway. Beaver Tail paused long enough to say, "All is ready. We will go into the woods with Meksem and Hugh."

Elan moved toward Chogan. "Let me take her."

He gently placed the babe in her arms, then rose in a smooth motion. With a final glance around the lodge, he met Telípe's gaze.

Though he didn't speak, his eyes said a great deal more than a simple farewell. He would be back, but first, he would do everything he could to make sure the wildcat had been taken care of permanently.

~

*C*hogan fell easily into the stealthy stride of the warriors as he followed Meksem. Beaver Tail treaded quietly behind him, and one of the white men, Hugh, fell at the rear of their line. He wasn't the loudest white man Chogan had ever heard walk through the woods, but he clearly hadn't practiced the art of silence from his youngest days as the rest of them had. As long as he didn't scare away the wildcat before they could spot its sign, Chogan didn't let himself be distracted by the noise.

He had too many other things to focus on. Meksem seemed a capable leader and good at spotting signs, but his position required he notice anything she missed.

Everything she missed.

He strained with all his senses, listening for the smallest scrape of the cat's rough pad on bark. Sniffing the breeze for the sour scent male wildcats sometimes left behind. Spotting any claw mark on a branch or a place where dried leaves had been crunched.

Though this wildcat had lived so long by staying hidden, it must have left a mark somewhere. They simply had to find it.

Of course, they weren't searching in the direction the cat had escaped after the river attack. In fact, they were moving the opposite way. But Beaver Tail said each of the groups was assigned a territory to cover, fanning out away from the village. This was their assigned section, maybe given to this haphazard group—half comprised of untrusted and untried strangers—because it seemed the least likely area the cat would be.

But something in Chogan's instincts told him this was an important territory. If he wasn't mistaken, they were nearing the area he'd first heard the two wildcats fighting as he'd been setting up camp the night of his arrival. He'd seen more than a few signs of the animal in this section during the time he'd been hunting it, before his sickness.

Maybe the beast wasn't here now, but it was possible they'd find its lair. And maybe—if they were attentive enough—they would be here when it returned.

Yet the farther they pushed with no sign of the cat, the more his belly knotted. They spread out, keeping within occasional sight of each other but in a wide enough line to stretch across the width of the territory they'd been assigned.

The sun hung only one finger above the western horizon by the time a soft call from Beaver Tail signaled they should stop and gather around him.

Chogan did his best not to show his frustration, but some of it surely crept onto his face. The others wore grim expressions, too, as the four of them gathered in a circle.

Beaver Tail pointed to two boulders stacked one on the other next to a cliff overhang. "This is as far as Uyítpe said to go. Have you seen any sign?"

Meksem shook her head, her mouth forming a tight line.

Hugh spoke broken Blackfoot and accompanied his words with signs. "Only claw marks on a tree. Old."

Then Beaver Tail turned to Chogan.

"The same. Claw marks from many sleeps ago. Nothing fresh." It made no sense they'd not seen recent sign. When he camped at the black rock, he'd heard the animal's cries often near this area.

Beaver Tail nodded. "We turn back then and follow different paths this time."

Objection flared in Chogan's chest, and he started to shake his head. He wouldn't stop looking until they found something to point them in the right direction.

Maybe Beaver Tail guessed his thoughts, for the man raised a staying hand. "We'll cover our area again, back and forth, until first light or until we've received word the cat is found."

Chogan clamped his mouth shut. At least the man didn't plan to return to the village now. By first light, they could search this stretch at least once more, maybe twice. Though they'd have to move slower in the dark in order to not miss something important.

As Chogan chose a new path to follow for this return trip, he honed his senses even tighter. He couldn't miss anything, not even a stray hair.

If they didn't catch the wildcat this night, who knew which life would be in danger next.

CHAPTER 11

Telípe stood outside their lodge door in the gray morning light as bands of warriors began to straggle in. She'd slept little in the night. The babes had awakened more often than their normal feeding times, and her brother had been restless with his pain.

Just now when she'd checked him, his body felt warmer than usual. Not a good sign. Elan had reminded her of another root that aided healing, especially when wounds brought on fever. But Telípe had not been able to locate it in the village stores. She knew what grape root looked like growing wild though. If she could be allowed out to look along the riverbank, she was sure she could find some.

But the chief had given strict instructions that no one was to leave the village, not until the warriors returned with the wild-cat's carcass.

She studied each person approaching in the dim light, seeking out both the giant body of a wildcat and the broad shoulders that always made her heart leap. So far, neither appeared through the morning haze.

As long as the lodge stayed quiet, she could stand here and

watch, for she desperately longed to see Chogan safe. The others, too, of course—Meksem, Beaver Tail, and Hugh, who'd searched with Chogan. And every other man who'd left from the village.

But then her eyes made out that familiar form. Her heart did its usual happy jump. Her feet started forward without conscious thought.

At the edge of the village, she made herself stop and wait. None of the wives were rushing out to meet their husbands. She would look foolish leaving to meet this brave who, as far as the others were aware, she barely knew.

But she *did* know him. Her heart had connected with him so strongly since he returned across the mountains. They needed time to learn more about each other, but her heart already knew his nature. His goodness.

Beside Chogan trudged Beaver Tail. On his other side and back a little, Hugh stumbled forward, weariness cloaking his shoulders more than the others. They must all be exhausted. She'd not managed much sleep, but these braves would've had none at all.

Meksem, of course, walked a little ahead of their group. Her sister wouldn't show exhaustion until her dying breath. Telípe couldn't help but envy that strength. Though the intensity that drove Meksem to that point had been almost painful to watch at times.

Yet how wonderful it must be to have such finely honed aim toward a goal. The determination to achieve what she sought, no matter what stood in the way.

Maybe Telípe's mind was muddled from lack of sleep—both last night and every other night since the babes were born. Her focus was as far from honed as it had been in a long time. The little ones pulled her in so many directions.

At last, Meksem and the others reached her, and the disappointment on their faces showed how their hunt had gone.

Meksem was the first to break the silence. "Have any of the others brought news?"

Telípe hesitated. Maybe she should have been focused on learning that instead of seeking out Chogan. She slipped a glance toward him but then tugged her gaze back to her sister. "I've not heard anything, but not everyone is back yet." That was true, and it didn't make her sound so empty-headed.

Meksem nodded, then started forward. "I'll find Uyítpe. He'll know if anything has been learned."

Telípe stepped aside for her sister to pass, then turned and fell into step with Chogan and the other two men as they followed Meksem.

Chogan glanced sideways at her. "Your brother?"

Pain twisted her belly. "He didn't rest well. Much pain and some fever this morning." She could give no promise of the outcome. These next few days would tell more.

The sadness in Chogan's eyes pressed even harder on her. These weren't his people. Why should he spend all night hunting for an animal who threatened their village? This was not his burden to bear.

Yet he gladly took it on himself. Simply because he wanted to help? He'd been cast out of his own village. Was he seeking another? Did *she* have anything to do with his presence here?

With everything in her, she wanted that answer to be *yes*. But how could she be so vain? There was something between them—she was fairly sure he felt it. But enough for him to change his plans because of her?

Maybe if they spent time alone, she could eventually learn the answers.

But this was not that time.

When they passed by her brother's lodge, she peered inside to see if she was needed there. Both babes still slept, a wonder in itself. Maybe that extra feeding in the night helped them rest longer now.

Her brother's wife knelt by the fire, and Gezíu seemed to finally be resting, even in his pain. Maybe it would be all right to follow Chogan and hear what the others had found about the wildcat. She could keep an ear tuned for her babies' cries.

As she straightened and turned to catch up with Chogan and the others, he paused and watched her approach. She took long strides to reach him, then fell into stride beside him again.

His hand brushed the small of her back. A quick touch, but the connection swept through her. It felt as though he wanted her beside him. To be wanted felt good, and by *this* man—even better.

She was wanted by her babes, and being their mother fulfilled a deep longing inside her. But they always *needed* something from her. At Chogan's side, she didn't always have to give. With him, she could take—borrow strength from him, enjoy his friendship. Enjoy the way he made her feel special. Set apart from others.

She'd never been special. The middle child, stretched between Meksem—from their mother's first family—and her brothers, who always needed something from her.

As they approached the gathering of braves, the somber faces around her pulled her back to the present. A few women from the village came with their men, probably as relieved to see everyone returned safely as she was.

One face about a dozen strides away stood out from the rest, the glare he sent their direction making Telípe want to step back out of his line of sight. Except that glower wasn't aimed at her. Pisákas looked like he wanted to ram a spear through Chogan. Because Chogan was being allowed to mingle with their people now? Or because he stood beside her. She wasn't Pisákas's wife—far from it. And maybe that fact was what kept the man from charging Chogan.

. . .

*J*n front of them, Uyítpe made a sound to silence the murmurs in the group. Telípe did her best to focus on him and ignore Pisákas. "Our hunt this night was not successful, but we have learned the cat still lives. He still intends danger for our people. We have tracked in a half circle around the village. We have found where he beds down. Even now, warriors stand guard there to catch him."

Uyítpe's voice strengthened, echoing through the village, surely waking those who still slept. Mostly the grandmothers and children, by this time of morning. "No one is to leave the village without immediate need until the cat is killed. When the women go to the river, there are to be two braves for every two people. We will station guards around the edge of our camp. More groups of warriors will be sent out to watch over the cat's nest. Until your turn comes for one of these jobs, you should rest and prepare for battle against this predator."

The man again called out names, assigning those names to duties.

Beside her, she could feel the tension in Chogan's body as he listened. Meksem's name was called as one of the warriors who would escort the women to the river. Pisákas's too. Hopefully that would keep him busy for a while.

Water would be the primary need of the villagers. Since it was mid-summer, they would have enough food saved to last a few days at least. But what of the grape root for her brother? Did she dare raise her hand and ask?

She had to.

At first, she lifted her hand tentatively. But she couldn't be a cautious maiden. So she raised her hand fully and waved to gain Uyítpe's attention. When he looked her way, she lifted her voice loud enough to reach him. "My brother needs a root to help with his healing. We think it might be found by the river to the north. May I go look for it?"

Uyítpe narrowed his eyes, maybe weighing the importance of her need. Or maybe determining who best should accompany her. At last, he nodded. "Beaver Tail and Chogan will go with you as guards."

Her weary face wanted to pull into a smile, but she simply nodded. "Thank you."

The group separated shortly after, each person going to their assigned duties. Meksem strode away to gather the braves assigned to her. Thankfully, she took charge of Pisákas first.

Beaver Tail and Chogan turned to Telípe. Weariness showed in both their eyes, but Chogan spoke first. "You are ready to go now to find this root?"

These men needed rest before she forced them back to work. She shook her head. "I need to attend the babes and help with my brother first. Rest a while, and I'll send for you when I'm ready." They couldn't wait too long, for Gezíu needed the medicine. But a nap should help them at least a little.

~

The chaos had returned to their family lodge. Telípe had to hold in a grunt of frustration as the noise grew louder and louder. Her youngest brother didn't stay confined easily, and he'd long ago tired of playing with his stones and practicing with his bow.

Her own babes seemed to feed on his discontent, fussing and squirming no matter how she positioned them. She fed both little ones for a long time, but neither seemed eager to fall asleep again.

She'd barely moved to the fire to scoop out portions of gruel for the grandmother and herself before Kapskáps began to fuss and act as though she was still hungry. Lately, the child never seemed to get enough.

After she'd fed the babe once more and done everything

necessary in the lodge, she finally strapped Éisnin in the cradle-board and scooped up her twin.

As she lifted Kapskáps to her shoulder, she patted her back. "I won't be able to call you the smaller babe much longer, will I? You're almost as long as your sister." The child responded with a belch, then stiffened her back as though eager to get moving.

Normally, Telípe might have chuckled at her daughter's antics, but her patience had rubbed thin. With a final glance around the lodge to make sure her sister-in-law could manage, she met Ámtiz's gaze. The woman nodded, her eyes saying she would make sure all was well. How many times had Telípe silently thanked her brother for marrying this woman, this enduring source of patience?

After returning a nod of thanks, Telípe headed through the doorway. The mist from earlier still hovered in the air, and tiny drops of rain settled on her face as she moved to the next lodge, where Chogan and Beaver Tail stayed. Rain today, of all things? Maybe they could find a grape bush and return before the showers came in earnest.

As she ducked inside, she glanced around the large circle. Though so many slept here, the women kept the place tidy, rolling up most of the bed pallets during the day.

Chogan sat on one of the rolled bundles, tying on his tall moccasins, and Beaver Tail loaded arrows into a quiver with Susanna at his side.

Colette stood when Telípe entered, her heavy belly making her movements slow. But she managed well, waddling forward with her hands out to take one of the babes. All the women here had offered to watch the twins while she was gone.

Telípe hesitated. Would Kapskáps be too much for this expectant mother to manage in her condition? But she didn't dare take either of the children out where they might encounter a wildcat. She couldn't endanger these innocent babes when willing hands were here to watch them.

Behind her, Elan stepped into the lodge. "You're ready to go out? Let me take one of the children. Do you remember how the branches of the grape bush look in the summer?"

Telípe nodded. "I remember." She and Elan had both grown up here, though Elan had been a few years older. Meksem's age.

Elan's brow furrowed before she moved around behind Telípe to take the cradleboard from her back. "I don't think there's any left in the place you and I went when you were little. But I hope farther upriver. Do you want me to go instead?"

Disappointment pressed through Telípe. No. She wanted to go. She needed time outside of lodge walls to clear her mind. And time with the two Blackfoot braves—one in particular— had been calling to her every moment since the chief had ordered them to go with her.

Telípe shook her head. "We'll go quickly. I just fed the babes, and Kapskáps ate twice. They should nap soon, and I'll be back before they need to eat again."

Elan didn't question further. Maybe she remembered a new mother's need for a few moments away from her newborns.

A new thought slipped in, and Telípe couldn't help a quick glance at Elan's middle. She and Joel had been married since the middle of winter. Might there be a child growing inside her? How would Elan feel about it when there was? She could still remember the woman's grief when her first husband and daughter were killed in a bear attack. The haunting in her eyes had brought tears to Telípe more than once.

Now that she had her own daughters, these sweet babes she would give her life to protect, she couldn't begin to imagine how deep Elan's grief had been.

As Chogan and Beaver Tail approached, she turned her focus to them. Chogan's gaze met hers, his eyes searching her expression. "You're ready?"

She nodded. "We need to go quickly."

CHAPTER 12

Felípe left the camp with the two braves, and they fell into step across the open land, Chogan on her left and Beaver Tail on her right. She'd never felt so protected as she did in this moment. Their strength fed through her, infusing her with confidence.

When they reached the first group of bushes along the river's edge, she scanned the undergrowth. "The grape bush should have wide leaves like this one, but so wide they're almost a circle with only a point on one end. I've never seen it grow taller than this." She held her hand out, level with her waist. "Its branches are spindly, almost like a sapling tree but not as thick."

As she searched for the branches she described, they moved along the river's bank. A glance at both men showed they weren't helping much with her search. Each man scanned the area around them, their gazes keen. An intensity surrounded Chogan so thick that he seemed almost like a wildcat himself, coiled and ready to spring.

Part of her wanted to touch his arm, to ease his tension. But he looked as though a single brush might make him jump.

Was it exhaustion that made him so tense? Or did something

else drive him to find the cat? Perhaps simply the duty he felt to ensure her safety. That sounded exactly like the Chogan she'd come to know.

As they walked, she asked about where they'd hunted in the night. Beaver Tail answered most of her questions, his responses complete yet without any extra detail. Exhaustion might be weighing heavily on him as well. But he was also a brave, one she was only now coming to know. It made sense he wouldn't be comfortable with small talk.

Silence slipped over them as they walked farther and farther upstream. It was hard to tell how far the sun had moved up in the sky, for thick clouds covered the expanse overhead. At least the raindrops had ceased, though it looked as if they might resume any minute.

They had to find a grape bush soon. They would need to turn around soon, or the babes would be hungry before she returned. Maybe she should have sent Elan instead. The thought of her wee ones crying, inconsolable because of the gnawing in their bellies, brought the burn of tears to her own eyes. She'd been far too apt to cry lately. Perhaps the lack of a full night's sleep made the tears rise so quickly.

She peered through every grouping of brush on their side of the river and continually glanced across the water to see what grew on that shore. Her body became more tense the farther they went. She could almost hear her babes' cries in her mind.

Just as she'd decided they had to turn back, a plant across the river caught her notice.

Stepping to the edge of the bank, she strained to see better. Large rocks littered the water, sending the current into a rushing rapid that sounded loud in her ears, drowning out the brisk beat in her chest.

Was that a grape bush? She had to be sure before she chanced crossing the river. It had to be, though. From everything she could see, that looked exactly like the plant she remembered.

She turned back to Chogan and Beaver Tail. "I see it across the river. I'll go get what I need, and then we can start for the village."

Chogan shook his head. "I'll cross with you."

"We'll all cross." Beaver's voice sounded as determined as Chogan's.

She shrugged. "If you like."

Chogan started across first, leaping from one stone to the next. In the middle section, they would have to step into the water, which meant they'd all be walking back in wet moccasins. Not the worst fate, but not her favorite condition.

When Chogan had stepped across the first two rocks, she started behind him. Her legs weren't nearly as long as his, but she managed to make the jumps, with her foot slipping into the water only once.

He waded the two steps through the center of the river, the water surging around his legs. Before he climbed up onto the next rock, he stopped and turned, reaching out for her. She could manage through rivers as well as anyone, but she wouldn't refuse a chance to grasp his hand when offered.

She stepped from the rock into the rushing water. Though she'd been prepared for a swift current, this one pushed stronger than she'd expected. She swayed, then secured herself better against the push.

Chogan grasped her hand, his grip firm, a solid tree in the midst of a fierce wind. She let him pull her forward through the current.

When she reached the next rock, he climbed up, still gripping her hand, and pulled her up next to him. The stone was large enough to allow them both to stand, but just barely. He shifted her in front of him, her back to his chest, and everything inside her longed to lean against him. They were almost touching anyway. He clasped each of her elbows and spoke into her ear. "Let me go ahead in case it's slippery."

The warmth of his breath on her skin and the rumble of his voice sent a shiver through her that was impossible to withstand. He must've felt it with his palms cupping her arms. Did he have any idea how much he affected her? He might have realized at least a little, for his thumbs brushed the backs of her arms, a caress that nearly weakened her knees.

She swallowed, summoning everything she had to stand on her own, to lean forward so he could move past her. Beaver Tail was already coming, stepping down from the rock into the middle of the river. They all had to keep moving.

They only had two more rocks to cross before they reached shore, and she followed Chogan through the final steps. He reached to help her onto dry ground, though she didn't need it.

He probably knew she didn't need his help for that step. But he brushed his thumb across the top of her hand in a gentle caress before he finally released her, and they stepped back for Beaver to join them on the bank.

She blinked once to clear her mind and focus on the task before them. The grape bush.

She'd brought the pointed tool she used to harvest camas root, but this plant, with its long roots sprawling in all directions, wouldn't be nearly so easy to dig out. She knelt beside the bush and began digging.

Chogan stepped near. "Should I pull it out?"

She shook her head. "The roots are long and fragile. I'll have to dig them."

"I need to stand guard." His voice came low, almost regretful. Braves rarely dug in the dirt, but did he mean he would have helped her with this task? She'd never known a man desire so strongly to take others' burdens on himself.

She glanced up at him and nodded. "This work isn't hard."

Focusing on her digging, she took care not to nick even one

of the precious roots. They would cut these into tiny pieces and boil them in water until they could be mashed into a poultice for Gezíu's wounds. Would this one plant be enough? She eyed the size of the bush.

At the corner of her gaze, something moved.

Her mind registered the motion just as Beaver Tail fit an arrow into his bow and sent the tip soaring toward a massive creature. The wildcat was huge, even bigger than it'd seemed when it had attacked her brother. The beast sprang away from them at Beaver Tail's first movement, but the arrow struck its hip.

The animal somersaulted sideways, maybe from the force of the arrow's blow.

Telípe's heart surged into her throat as Chogan leapt forward. He held his blade poised in the air, ready to shove it into the cat's heart with a mighty blow.

But the animal came out of its roll running. The arrow no longer poked from its hindquarters. The shaft must have broken during the animal's roll. The creature shot forward as if launched by a bowstring itself.

Chogan paused to fling his knife. The weapon struck the cat's tail, glancing off it before landing in the grass as the beast tore away.

He sprinted after the animal for several steps, but the cat soared from ground to rock to tree, disappearing within a few heartbeats. By the time they ran that same distance, the creature would be far beyond them.

Chogan slowed, scooped up his knife, then turned and walked toward them, shoulders sagging under the weight of his disappointment and exhaustion. If only she could close the distance between them and slip herself under his arm, wrapping her hands around his waist and offering what support she had.

But she wasn't free to do that. She didn't belong to this brave.

"At least we know where he is." Beaver Tail's voice hung with the same frustration weighing Chogan's body.

Chogan nodded but didn't speak. When he reached them, he turned and glanced behind him, scanning for the cat once more. But then he turned back, knelt by the grape bush, and took up Telípe's digging tool. As though he *had* to do something to help.

She knelt beside him and used her hands to extract the roots as Chogan loosened the dirt around each one. She would've told him to be careful not to cut the roots, but that knowledge seemed innate within him. He worked with more care than even she had managed.

Together, they soon had the full bush extracted from the ground. Chogan stood and reached a hand to help her up. His eyes showed weariness, yet his grip was strong. After she rose, he scanned their surroundings, his gaze turning sharp. Even as they crossed the river, his watchfulness never ceased. No wildcat would be a match for this warrior.

~

"Come eat with us, Telípe. Time outside will do you good."

Elan's gentle pleading tugged at Telípe. This sweet woman had been a good friend to Meksem through the years, not to mention how much she'd helped Telípe in childbirth and afterward with the babes. And now she was helping with Gezíu's care.

Telípe studied her middle brother once more as he lay on his sickbed. They'd freshened the grape root poultice, and the grandmother never strayed far from the lad. His body was still warmer than it should be, but that didn't seem to have worsened throughout the day. Maybe she wouldn't be missed if she joined Elan's and her friends for a meal around their outside campfire.

She turned back to her friend and nodded. "I'll need to bring the babes."

"Of course." Elan smiled. "We have lots of hands eager to hold them."

Telípe glanced toward the stew pot where Ámtiz worked. It held only enough for their family. Her mind scrambled for what she could bring.

But maybe Elan heard her thoughts. "Colette, Otskai, and Susanna have been cooking all afternoon. Please don't bring anything. We've enough for two meals."

Relief washed through her. If she had her own lodge, with only herself and her babes to worry about, she might have had extra to bring. But with all of these people coming in and out, food never seemed to last long.

She sent Elan a smile. "Thank you."

She gathered up Kapskáps, and Elan lifted Éisnin. Then they stepped outside to the scent of woodsmoke drifting through the air. Though the summer sun wouldn't set for a while, a blaze had been lit in front of Elan's lodge. Several people sat around it, two of them kneeling near enough to be working on the food. The others seemed to be enjoying conversation.

As Telípe and Elan approached, Telípe's gaze searched for Chogan's form. The only men in the group who'd gathered so far were Caleb and Louis, the younger of the two Frenchmen who'd come with Colette. Were the other men still sleeping? Elan had said they'd all either finished their guard duty for the day or weren't scheduled to take their turn until the morning watch.

Maybe the scent of food and sounds of conversation would awaken Chogan if he still slept.

But that wasn't a good line of thought. He needed the rest. He could eat when his body recovered its strength.

Colette reached for Éisnin before Telípe could sit. "I'm sure your hands are tired of holding babies." She used a mixture of

Nimiipuu and English, which required a moment for Telípe to interpret.

Once the words came clear, Telípe offered a smile and handed her over.

"Sit and tell us how your brother fares. Is the heat inside him growing cooler?" Otskai's look hung thick with concern.

Telípe sat beside Elan, then reached to take Éisnin. Elan waved her hand away. The babe was nestled in the crook of her arm and lap, quiet for once.

So Telípe turned her focus to answer Otskai. "He grows no worse. Ámtiz's grandmother rarely leaves his side, and I hope the grape root is working even more as time passes."

Susanna turned a frown on her. "Do you think you'll need more? Maybe the braves will plan a hunting trip to that area to look for the cat again, and they can bring back more of the bush for you." She lifted her focus to the lodge door as Beaver Tail stepped out.

The tender expression that passed between them tightened Telípe's belly. The man looked like he'd awakened recently, and he strode directly to his wife, kneeling beside her in a position that blocked them from Telípe's view.

She turned aside anyway. She'd never seen two people so obviously in love as this pair—well, other than Elan and Joel. And Caleb and Otskai. Even Meksem, for all her fierce expressions, melted when Adam drew near. He had an easy-going manner that blended perfectly with her sister's warrior ways.

Then another figure stepped from the lodge, drawing Telípe's gaze and sending her heart fluttering.

Chogan.

elípe's belly flipped as Chogan's eyes found her, a grin twinkling in them. Then his expression softened as his gaze dropped to her arms, then sideways to Elan as he sought out both babes. The tenderness on his face pressed tightness in her chest.

He stepped toward Telípe but then paused at Elan's side and bent low to see Kapskáps, slipping his large, calloused finger within her tiny grip. The babe looked at him, watching him as he studied her. "Hello, my strong one. You've grown since this morning." His voice rumbled softly, almost intimate as the babe watched him.

The sight and sound twisted through Telípe, love spreading within her for both of them—man and babe. Was it wrong to love this Blackfoot brave? Maybe that wasn't the emotion that dwelled within her yet, but she was quickly moving to that point. If she were to have any hope of stopping the love, she had to do it now. Had to distance herself from him. But did she want to?

Elan's voice broke through her confusion. "Do you want to hold her?" She looked at Chogan, brows raised.

His throat worked. His gaze lifted to Telípe, his eyes asking permission. How could she say no? She dipped her chin in a nod.

As Chogan took the babe from Elan's hands and lifted her to the cradle of his arm, Telípe's body reacted exactly the way she'd feared. The love within her welled up so rich and full, tears burned her eyes.

*C*hogan kept his gaze focused on the child as he moved around Elan to Telípe's other side. He glanced at Telípe before shifting his attention back to the babe as he lowered himself to sit beside her.

Emotion clogged her throat as she watched them. And Kapskáps seemed equally riveted on Chogan's face.

She couldn't have said how long they sat like that. The murmur of voices sounded from the others, but nothing loud enough to break through the beauty of the moment.

At last, words from others began to slip in. Someone must have asked about Meksem, and Adam responded with, "She's coming soon. She remembered one more thing to tell the chief. Something she saw by the river, I think." Adam's Nimiiputimpt had improved quite a bit since Telípe had first met him back in the winter.

Conversation flowed freely among the group, sometimes in Nimiiputimpt, sometimes in English. And she couldn't be certain, but it seemed like every so often, a bit of the French tongue slipped in. There was such a mix of nationalities and languages represented in this group that it was a wonder anyone could follow along. Often, Elan or Beaver Tail would lean forward and translate something said into a language the rest could understand.

By the time Meksem, French, and Hugh arrived, bowls of stew were being passed around. Elan was right that the women had cooked far more than enough to feed even this large group.

Talk quieted as hungry bellies were filled. When Caleb placed his empty dish in front of him, he sent a raised-brow grin toward French. "Have you and Colette decided when you'll marry?"

French and Colette sat on the opposite side of the fire as Telípe, so she couldn't see the detail of their faces well. But the dip of Colette's chin as she glanced sideways at her intended showed the embarrassment Telípe probably would've felt at such a bold question.

French's white teeth flashed in a grin as he slipped his hand behind her back. "Soon. We were thinking tomorrow, but it might be better to wait until that mountain cat's caught and we're allowed out of the village." He turned his smile on Colette, and a long gaze passed between them. That same sweetness she'd seen earlier with Beaver Tail and Susanna.

She'd seen so few examples of that kind of love, she'd never really thought it was something she could find for herself. Yet each of the couples around this campfire seemed to have managed it. Would such a life be possible for her? She could almost imagine it with the tall brave sitting beside her.

But how did one manage to find not only that initial love, but something with strength to last a lifetime? From what she'd heard of their stories, Beaver Tail and Susanna had been the first in this group to find each other and marry. They didn't seem tired of each other at all. In fact, their love seemed deeper, even more seasoned and mature than these others.

Was there a secret to achieving that? Some special require- ment in one or both people? Maybe she could find the courage to ask Susanna when they were alone.

~

*T*his group of people possessed something special.

Chogan had never felt such a kinship as what united these friends. They came from so many tribes, some pale skin and some dark, yet not even the barrier of multiple languages could stop their camaraderie. The two brothers from Canada, Hugh and Louis, didn't seem to have quite become part of the band yet, although from the occasional surprise or confusion in their expressions, it seemed like their reticence might be more on their side. From what he could tell, the rest of the group accepted them without question.

Chogan could well understand what those Frenchmen felt. He wasn't quite sure how to interact with these people. But he knew one thing deep inside him. He *wanted* to be part. Wanted to be accepted as a brother—a member of this unique family.

He glanced at Telípe, as he had so many times throughout the evening. Was she part of them or not? Sometimes, with the easiness between her and Meksem or Elan, she seemed comfortable and included.

But when one of the men spoke—especially the white men— she regarded him with that same curiosity Hugh and Louis showed, an expression that marked her as an outsider looking in.

Did she simply not know them well enough? Or was she shy, hesitant to join fully in the banter? Maybe even insecure about whether or not she would be accepted.

Not a crumb of that insecurity would be warranted. Who wouldn't welcome Telípe? Her sweet spirit, the way she didn't shirk hard work when someone needed her. And most of all, her desire to champion those she believed in as she had with him—twice now.

But he was finally proving himself. The village had eased their restrictions on him and had mostly given him into the care of Beaver Tail. The time spent with that brave had increased

Chogan's respect for him more each day. There was only one man in the village who seemed to go out of his way to show his disdain for Chogan. The fellow who'd spoken against his presence when Meksem first brought Chogan in.

He'd not learned the man's name yet, but the glares were hard to miss. A little more subtle were the possessive gazes toward Telípe, but Chogan had seen enough to know jealousy lay near the root of the man's dislike.

Was the jealousy warranted? He glanced sideways at Telípe, taking in her beauty, the sweet expression that mirrored the goodness inside her. Whether she felt anything for him or not, he could no longer deny how much this woman had crept inside him and taken over his heart.

A smile brightened her face, her white teeth flashed in the dusky light. Someone must have told a joke for chuckles rumbled through those around the fire. He forced his attention to the others.

Maybe, if he continued to prove himself trustworthy and capable, he might one day be accepted into this unlikely group. The yearning for that very thing was so strong it scared him. What if he did something to lose this family just like he'd lost the clan he'd been born into?

"Who all has guard duty in the morning?" Adam's question broke through Chogan's thoughts. Adam spoke in Nimiiputimpt, then translated into English for the others in the group. Chogan knew a smattering of English—enough to trade, but not much more. He understood even less French than that.

That was another thing Beaver Tail excelled in. He seemed fluent in not only Blackfoot, English, and Nimiiputimpt, but he also spoke French and Shoshone well enough to communicate. And of course, he could sign as well as he could speak his native tongue.

Pressing down the surge of jealousy, Chogan focused on translating Meksem's response. "Louis and French will go with the women to the river. Beaver Tail and Chogan will go with you and me as part of the group tracking north to hunt the cat."

"Good." Susanna turned to her husband and Chogan. "When you're traveling north, look for more grape root. Telípe said she would need more for her brother's wounds."

Chogan glanced at Telípe. "How many bushes do you think?"

Her expression brightened with hope, yet she seemed to hesitate. "One would be helpful. Two even more so."

He raised his brows at her. "And three even better?"

A smile illuminated her eyes. "Yes."

Then he'd do his best to bring back four grape bushes for her. In fact, he'd bring back the moon if he could manage it.

Or at least, one oversized mountain cat.

❧

*C*hogan hadn't expected the Nimiipuu braves to be so capable. They didn't run the entire way after leaving the village at daylight that morning, but they moved quickly and quietly. He stayed with Beaver Tail, Meksem, and Adam on one side of the river. Four other braves from the village tracked on the opposite side. One way or another, they would find the wildcat on this journey. Though he strained for any sound or sign that would signal the cat's presence, he also watched for the bushes Telípe had described—leaves almost round, yet with a tiny point. A scraggly plant with branches not very full.

They reached the place where they'd crossed the river the morning before to harvest the first bush. But they kept moving. The landscape on both sides had more growth in this area. More chances to find the root. If he did locate it, should he stop to harvest the plant now and then catch up with the others? Or mark the place in his mind and come back for it?

Maybe the latter so he wouldn't be weighed down with

scraggly branches. Yet, who could say how long this hunt would go and where the animal's tracks would take them?

The sun had reached its peak as the land began to change around them. The prairie stretching on one side of the river was now marked with boulders, and the sides of the riverbank grew steep. Not as much underbrush here either.

He'd spotted one grape bush on the way and possibly one more on the opposite side of the river, though he'd been moving too fast to tell for sure. The group on the other bank had spotted muddy pawprints dried on one of the rocks beside the river that must have come the afternoon before.

There had been no sign of the cat on the bank where Chogan searched.

All they could do was press on, keeping every sense on alert, straining to hear or see or smell even the smallest sign. Thankfully, Pisákas seemed fully focused on finding the cat too, not acknowledging Chogan's presence at all.

The sun pierced so much hotter than it had in recent days. The peak of summer had finally arrived. Sweat ran in thick droplets down his chest and back, but that wasn't nearly enough to induce him to pull off his tunic. Neither Beaver Tail nor Adam stripped down, but even if they did, he wasn't ready to reveal his scars. Soon, his shirt grew damp enough to cool him. A small relief.

A movement in the distance captured his attention. He squinted at the distant outline as he raised a finger to point at it.

"Elk." Adam's voice came low yet hummed with excitement.

The tiny figures were too far away to see size, but he could make out at least six animals, perhaps more. A herd of that many would surely have a male. So much meat to stock up for winter. They couldn't pass up this chance.

He glanced at the others, who all stared at the distant herd. Across the river, the braves were looking that direction too, but from their position, they must not have been able to make out what the forms were.

He cupped his hands around his mouth to aim his voice and kept his tone just loud enough to reach them. "Elk herd."

Understanding settled over their expressions, and a bit of excitement too. Maybe the sport of the hunt lured them, or maybe the pleasure of providing for their families. The Nimiipuu seemed to exist mostly on smoked salmon and camas root. Meat like elk and deer and buffalo were a mainstay for his own people but seemed to be a treat for this village.

Chogan had to stop thinking of the Blackfoot as *his* people. He'd happily eat salmon and camas for the rest of his days if he were accepted into this village. Among these people.

With Telípe.

The group across the river found a place to ford and joined them. It didn't take long to discern they were all in agreement that as many elk should be taken as they could. A few braves could stay with the carcasses while the rest went back for horses to carry the meat.

They split up, some men moving across to the opposite side of the prairie where they could have access to the other side of the herd.

Chogan stayed by the river, ducking low behind the rocks and shrubs. They were downwind from the animals, which would help them get close before being noticed. In fact, the herd didn't seem aware of their presence. All of them held bow and arrow ready, arrows notched and drawn as they approached.

The bull jerked his head up first, raising a magnificent rack of antlers as his nostrils flared. The animals stood in the middle of the meadow, halfway between each set of braves.

Beaver Tail had his arrow pointed at the bull, and it appeared several from the other group did, as well. So Chogan moved his aim to a cow closer to the water.

At the first *twing* of an arrow flying, Chogan released his.

The point arced high and landed exactly where he'd aimed, in the chest of the cow. The moment he released the first arrow, he readied a second and launched it. Then a third, aiming farther back into the elk's gut. The animal stumbled forward two steps, then went down.

As the others aimed at their own animals, the three remaining elk sprinted away.

Chogan stood and eyed the outcome of the hunt. Four elk taken, including the bull. These would feed many families, both now and after the meat was smoked to keep through the winter.

The braves all gathered by the bull elk, and two men volunteered to run back to the village for horses. The rest of them would begin field dressing the animals. Not a job he enjoyed but necessary for survival.

Once the meat was loaded on the packhorses and they started south toward the village, maybe he could finally gather the bushes Telípe needed. Another group would have to be sent out to find the cat. This hunt hadn't been a total loss—far from it. Quite a coup in most people's opinion—but the threat of the wildcat still hung heavily over them.

If the animal had come this far north, did that mean it had shifted his territory and would no longer be a threat to the village?

Maybe. But Chogan's instincts told him not to rely on that hope.

CHAPTER 14

*T*he sounds of boys wrestling and laughing carried from outside the lodge as Telípe bent over her middle brother's ravaged body. Ámtiz had taken her youngest brother to play with Pisákas's little boy—an effort to wear off energy for both the lads. Staying pent-up in the village was wearing on them all, especially the children.

Yet those concerns stayed far back in the recesses of Telípe's mind as worry for Gezíu crowded to the forefront. Every time the fever seemed to lessen, it came back again with a vengeance, rising even higher than before. She and the grandmother were doing their best to cool the lad with wet cloths. Susanna had given them strips of woven blankets, which worked much better than leather to soak up the water and drip it over her brother's burning skin. Yet every effort helped only a little, not enough to overcome the torment of the injuries.

One of the wounds on his shoulder had begun to fester, turning bright red and swelling, gray pus oozing from the scratch. A claw mark beside that had swollen even more, yet the skin had already adhered together, the center of the wound turning a dark gray. Was pus building inside?

Which was better, for the mess to ooze out or for the skin to close? She had a feeling the first would help him heal, dispelling the poisons.

Should she do something to open up that wound that seemed to hold the festering inside? So much she didn't know. The grandmother didn't seem sure either. Perhaps Elan had experience with this.

Gezíu kept his eyes closed most of the time, either sleeping or restless. The times he did open his eyes, they held a glazed look. Was that pain? Or was it caused by whatever was happening in his body?

If only she wasn't so helpless to make him better. What else could she try?

Footsteps sounded behind her, and she glanced back as Colette and Elan stepped into the lodge. They each carried one of the babes, and from the way Kapskáps fussed in Colette's arms, it must be feeding time again. Éisnin had begun tucking her fist in her mouth when she was hungry, which kept her from crying for a while. If only Kapskáps could learn the same.

She would need to take the babes, but first, Telípe motioned the women over. "Have you seen a wound closed and swelling like this?" She pointed to the worst of the gashes.

Both women peered over her shoulder, so she moved aside and stood to take Éisnin from Elan first, then Kapskáps from Colette.

As she changed soiled wrappings in preparation to feed the girls, she eyed the two women who were speaking quietly between themselves.

At last, Elan turned, and her gaze took in both Telípe and the grandmother. "I have seen this once. We had a brave who was shot with a gun in battle. He began to grow better, then worsened very quickly. Thick brown liquid gathered under his wound and made it swell and fester. The healer opened the gash with a blade and pulled out the small black ball."

A shiver slid through Telípe at the thought of taking a knife blade to the wound. Gezíu jerked or cried out anytime she touched those places. She studied Elan's face. "Did he recover?"

Elan nodded. "After a time."

A small measure of relief slipped through her, but her belly still twisted at the thought of doing the act. Could she manage it? She could skin an animal and cut out the food parts without too much roiling in her belly. But slicing through her brother's angry skin might be more than...

"Perhaps Síkem will do it." The grandmother's voice rose among them, confident as she usually was in her new grandson's abilities. He'd done much for his wife's grandmother. Taking her in when her son passed, giving her a comfortable home with her granddaughter. Of course, she would have confidence in him.

But Telípe remembered too well the young boy Síkem had been who grew squeamish watching a deer be skinned. He'd turned away and retched more than once, although after the first time, he'd learned to hide himself in the trees before doing so lest he bear the ridicule again.

"I'll ask those in our lodge," Elan said. "Maybe someone there will feel up to the task. If not, I'll do it." The softening of her voice on those last words showed just how much she dreaded the thought.

Telípe couldn't let Elan bear the brunt of the awful job, especially with the screams that would surely come from the boy's pain.

Elan turned and stepped to the lodge door. "I'll speak with the others, then prepare a knife."

Colette settled down beside Gezíu and rubbed her fingers down the boy's uninjured arm in a manner that must be soothing. Yet her brow furrowed more the longer she sat there. At last, she turned to Telípe. "He really is warm."

Worry pressed harder in Telípe's chest. "Yes."

They spoke no more of their fears, but anxiety hung heavy in the smoky air of the lodge. As the babes nursed, her gaze wandered to the grandmother. Having her and Ámtiz here to help with the boys had been a gift.

Had her brother and his young wife ever enjoyed time in an empty lodge? The younger boys had been here even before their marriage. Perhaps once all the chaos settled, Telípe could offer the man and wife some time to themselves.

When the babes finished nursing, both fell asleep, as was their usual routine at this time of day.

Telípe laid them on their fur and stood, rubbing at the sore spots on her shoulders that usually came from the weight of holding both infants. She glanced from the grandmother to Colette. The older woman stared at Gezíu's face, as she'd been doing almost the entire time Telípe fed the babes. She seemed almost to be in a trance. From worry? Or did she petition the great spirit?

Maybe they should ask Meksem to pray to her new God.

Colette met Telípe's gaze, and Telípe dropped her voice to a whisper. "I'm going outside for a moment." A breath of fresh air would give her time to clear her mind of the sadness pulsing through her.

Colette offered a small smile as she glanced towards the babes. "I'll stay here." Having so many friends around really helped lighten the burden. In the grandmother's dazed condition, Telípe wasn't certain she would be able to care for the little ones if they awoke.

Telípe sent her a grateful nod, then turned toward the daylight streaming around the edges of the door flap. Stepping out of the lodge felt like entering another world, one bright and hopeful without the haze of smoke and the tension clogging the air.

A figure standing at the next lodge over caught her attention, and her heart did the happy leap it always performed when she glimpsed Chogan.

He stepped toward her, his gaze roaming her face, seeking out her thoughts and feelings. Those eyes—they made her want to move toward him and step into his arms. What would it feel like to be wrapped in his strength? To have someone else to bear the weight of her fears and worries?

Maybe he saw those thoughts on her face, for he moved closer. Only an arm length separated them, and with his height, she had to look up into his face.

He studied her, and for a long moment, neither of them spoke. Then he motioned toward the path leading to the edge of camp. "Would you walk with me?"

Again her heart leaped. She desperately wanted time away. And even more than that, her heart longed for time with *him*. Walking would help clear her mind—wipe away her troubles at least. Her thoughts never quite seemed sharp with this man nearby, though.

They fell into step together. The route they took led them between several lodges, but they reached the edge of the camp far too soon.

Telípe paused, as did the tall brave beside her. "We aren't supposed to leave." Though the thought of shedding the restrictions of the village called to her.

Chogan motioned along the length of the camp toward the river. "We can stay by the outer edge."

Telípe turned that way. This would be better than nothing, though they were likely to be seen by many in the village. Tongues may wag. But then, she'd done more than one thing that shocked those around her.

She'd never been able to resist reaching out to those at the outer fringes. Those who didn't quite conform to the model their neighbors expected. Meksem had been one such case—the only child of her Salish father before he passed away, at which time her mother moved her back to this village. Chogan too, the time she'd stood between him and her sister's blade when Meksem came to free her from the Blackfoot kidnapping party.

So, no. She didn't mind doing something as simple as walking with a man the villagers didn't quite trust. The more she'd learned of his character, the more she'd come to trust him with everything she possessed.

Even her heart? The thought sent a frisson of fear through her. But she couldn't deny it. The man was working closer and closer to that spot each day.

As the light breeze ruffled her braids, cooling the sweat at the base of her neck, Telípe inhaled a chest-filling breath.

Chogan had been quiet for a while, and she glanced at him to see if she could gauge his thoughts from his expression. His brow was furrowed, his gaze locked on the ground in front of them as though his mind was far away.

He must've felt her looking, for he glanced her way and offered a sad smile. "Elan told us of your brother, of the poison festering under his skin."

The cloud of worry she'd left behind slipped around her again. "It won't be easy. The entire area is bright red and swollen, and the center where the claw struck is turning gray. He cries out at the lightest touch. But I think it must be done."

Chogan nodded, his face twisting in a look of pained determination. "He may not live if we don't. My sister died of wounds that festered. When the poison builds up too strongly beneath the skin, it moves through the entire body. After that, there will be little time left."

Telípe's chest squeezed as though a fist clenched so tightly that no air could pass in or out. "Your sister?"

He nodded, his mouth pinching. "I was twelve summers old when she died."

The pain he must have endured made her own body ache. Would her brother suffer the same outcome?

"The one other time I've seen wounds fester and swell with poison, a knife was used to cut open the angry skin and release the bad inside. The wound healed, though there was always a scar."

Something in his words, his tone, made her seek out the look on his face. There was a bitterness. A tension that spoke of a wound still raw—though this unhealed gash wasn't in the flesh. His expression revealed no details, but the way he no longer met her gaze meant something.

She laid her fingers on his arm. "Were you the one with the wound? Or the one wielding the knife?"

Pain flashed across his face, and he finally met her gaze. "The claws of a bear scraped my side. I should have recovered quickly, but the poison festered, and the fever came." He slowed, then stopped walking completely and reached for the tail of his buckskin frock. He lifted the left side only enough to show a sliver of skin, but the long line of scarring stole a gasp from her. The mark was outlined in blood red, with the inner skin lighter and puckered. That must have been painful.

Chogan dropped his shirttail and started forward again, his walk faster now than before. As though he were trying to run away from the conversation. Or maybe the memory.

She lengthened her stride to stay with him and didn't press for more. Though there must be a great more to that memory than what he'd shared. More pain than the gash itself.

At last, his stride settled, and he seemed to come back to the present. They'd nearly reached the edge of the village, and the river lay only a few strides ahead. This wasn't the clear section where the women went to retrieve drinking water, but the slower moving flow that tended to cloud with mud. Still, it offered a more pleasant view than the rows and rows of lodges.

At the corner of the camp, Chogan began to turn, but she motioned to the water. "I think we're safe to walk to the bank."

She glanced at him and offered a smile. "You're here to protect me, after all."

His brow wrinkled, and his expression grew concerned. "You don't think the chief would object?"

A new wave of appreciation for this man washed through her. How could anyone who came to know him not realize the depth of his integrity?

She stopped moving forward, staying there at the edge of camp. "We can just stand here then. The breeze that flows along the river feels good." She truly didn't think the chief would mind if they walked the final steps to the river, but she wouldn't put Chogan in danger of receiving anyone's anger for something as small as this. Nor did she want to be the one to make him go against his conscience.

Quiet sank over them once more, and she lifted her face to the breeze. At last, the gentle rumble of Chogan's voice sounded beside her. "I will do what I can to help your brother and cut the poison out of his wounds. If you wish me to."

Her heart lifted at the statement, and at the sacrifice he was willing to make. But those last few words he tacked on sounded almost like an apology for offering, as if he were giving her an easy way to decline.

She turned to face him, raising her chin so their gazes locked. "I don't want to make it hard on you. But if you think you can help my brother, please do."

Something shifted in his eyes. She couldn't read exactly what, but some of the pain seemed to ease away. He nodded, and his throat worked. "We should do it now then."

But he didn't look away. Didn't turn and stride back to the lodge.

His gaze held hers, stealing her breath, searing the moisture from her mouth with its intensity. Drawing her closer, so she couldn't have resisted the hold of his eyes if she wanted to.

But she didn't want to. Every part of her craved for him to lean down and press his lips to hers.

Then he blinked, and he seemed to force himself to look away. Disappointment flooded through her, and the sting of tears burned her eyes. This was no time for her emotions to run rampant.

She glanced around to distract herself, to bring herself back to their surroundings.

And they *were* surrounded. With the village beside them carrying on in its normal happenings, a kiss would not have been private. In fact, a cluster of children stared at them from beside a lodge three rows in. They would surely have raised a ruckus if things had continued between her and Chogan.

She dared a glance at the man. He'd turned to face the river, but his eyes were closed. Thankful for his narrow escape? Working, as *she* was, to pull himself back together? If only she knew more about his thoughts and feelings toward her.

He must've felt her gaze, for he opened his eyes and looked back at her. The intensity from before was gone, replaced by a tinge of sadness. "We should go to your brother now."

Yes. She held in a sigh as they turned back the way they'd come. Gezíu needed help more than anything else right now. He had to be her focus.

Not the tall brave who'd once more offered to give of himself in order to help her and those she loved.

CHAPTER 15

*C*hogan couldn't let memories steal his focus, but he did need to remember how this should be done.

While he held his knife in the flame to burn off any impurities, he replayed his father's actions all those winters ago. He had to lock his jaw against the emotions that tried to rise, focusing only on the mental image of the blade and how his father had used it to sever the inflamed skin. He'd pierced a hole in the area most swollen, then worked the ugly brown fluid out. One section on the end remained swollen, so he'd again burned the blade to cleanse it and pierced the center of that place.

Pain rose up to his chest, to his throat, and cut off his air. He turned away, pushing back the memories and the stinging that even now haunted the wound on his side like a ghost.

The blade should be clean now, so he pulled it from the flame and turned to the boy. A glance at Beaver Tail and Caleb showed both men ready to hold the lad down. Chogan had asked that the rest leave the lodge. Both the sights and sounds of this operation would be painful.

Elan had offered to stay and help soothe the lad or be an extra set of hands. He'd allowed it, though maybe he shouldn't have. But she had such a gentle way with the weak and injured, and that compassion would be helpful now. Not to mention her savviness with wounds and illnesses.

For a moment, he'd thought Telípe would ask to stay. Her face had been hesitant, clenching the knot in his belly. But Éisnin had begun to fuss in her arms, and she'd finally turned to the lodge door. He couldn't have allowed the pain that watching this event would cause her.

Caleb cleared his throat, drawing everyone's focus to him. "Can we say a prayer first?"

Chogan froze. Pray to the great spirit? Or to the God he'd heard these people speak of? Were they the same? He glanced at Beaver Tail. The man had his head bowed, shadows hiding his face. Elan also had ducked her head, and her eyes appeared closed.

Caleb's strong voice began, "Father, thank You that You love Gezíu more than we can even imagine. Guide Chogan's hands. Give him wisdom and strength as he does this hard thing. Heal this boy completely. In Jesus's name, amen."

Caleb lifted his face and met Chogan's gaze with a nod. Something in his look offered encouragement, as though he really believed Chogan could do this, that maybe he was even the best person to do this. A weight slipped off his chest, and he inhaled an easier breath. Now for the task itself.

He bent over the lad's shoulder, holding the blade above the spot where he would pierce the angry welt. The entire shoulder had swollen to twice its usual size, and beneath the skin where he would puncture had begun to turn smoky black. Not the deep purple of a bruise, but the awful hue of death, almost like toes or fingers frozen to the point of falling off. If only that meant the boy wouldn't feel this pain.

But the opposite would be true.

Elan murmured soft words to the lad as she rested one hand on his cheek, the other brushing through his tousled hair. The boy seemed almost asleep. But the mumbled sound he'd offered a moment before showed he wasn't unconscious.

He would feel this agony.

Locking his jaw, Chogan steeled his nerves against any jerking from the boy and pressed the tip of the blade into the putrid flesh.

A long, agonizing howl ripped from Gezíu's throat.

The moment Chogan felt his knife penetrate the skin, he pulled back.

Gezíu's body stilled, his back not even rising with breath.

Air didn't pass through Chogan's throat either as he strained for a sign of life.

The only movement was the slow seeping of gray puss from the hole he'd punctured.

At last, the boy inhaled a long breath. A moan slipped out with the air.

Elan continued her quiet encouragement, bending low with her face almost pressed against the lad's hair. His eyes were open, tears streaming from them, though he made no more sound.

If only he could fade into unconsciousness so he wouldn't feel the rest of this.

Only whimpers slipped from Gezíu's mouth as Chogan used his lightest touch to work the poison up through the hole. The seepage would continue for a while—a day even—so he didn't need to get it all out now. He only needed to make sure there wasn't a pocket of poison closed off somewhere. He would do whatever he could not to put the lad through this ordeal again later. Better to have it all done now. His own nerves might not manage the second round either.

At last, the swelling in the shoulder had eased evenly enough he felt certain no poison had been sealed away. He drew away from the lad and took in his first deep breath since pressing the knife to the boy's flesh.

Beaver Tail and Caleb also pulled back, leaving Elan as the only one still bent low over the boy. Her words shifted to encouragement about the hard part being done. The lad's eyelids drifted shut. Maybe, finally, he could rest and his body begin to heal itself.

As Chogan stood and turned toward the door flap, his legs weakened so much they nearly buckled. He just had to make it back to their own lodge. Then he could sit and recover his strength.

A hand settled on his back, a firm touch that bolstered his own strength. "Well done, my friend." Beaver Tail's words were low enough not to disturb the boy.

On Chogan's other side, Caleb stepped close, resting his own massive hand on Chogan's other shoulder. "Yes. You did good."

With the encouragement of these two strong men, strength flowed back into his limbs. He looked from one to the other, soaking in the friendship they offered. "Thank you." The words didn't begin to say everything that swelled within him.

~

*C*hogan sat atop his bed pallet the next morning with a bite of camas cake in his mouth, the remaining piece in his hand, as he listened to the words Caleb read from the white man's book in his hand.

He spoke them in English first, then Elan translated into Nimiiputimpt, sometimes with Beaver Tail's help on phrasing. The interpretation should have made the reading choppy and hard to follow, but not with this group. Instead, they used the back-and-forth flow to add details and ask questions about the words Caleb read.

They seemed to do this every morning, though this was only the third time Chogan had been there to hear, since he'd been hunting the wildcat the two other mornings after he'd been released from being held prisoner.

The stories Caleb read drew him like nothing before. Not even the shaman's teachings when he was a boy had sprung to life like these did. Those had been hard to follow, with mystical words that didn't string together into concrete ideas in his mind, perhaps because he'd been a boy.

"'Then the Lord answered Job out of the whirlwind, and said, "Who is this that darkeneth counsel by words without knowledge? Gird up now thy loins like a man; for I will demand of thee, and answer thou me. Where wast thou when I laid the foundations of the earth? Declare, if thou hast understanding.""' Caleb's voice hummed with deep intensity, and Chogan could well imagine a mighty being rumbling the questions to this small man named Job.

Was the God who laid the foundations of the earth the same as the great spirit Chogan had been seeking?

Elan translated the words in Nimiiputimpt, then turned back to Caleb in the same language. "Why would God take the time to answer Job and reveal his power through words? Why not simply act to show everyone that he was sovereign?"

Beaver Tail murmured a quick translation of her words into English, but Caleb seemed to understand enough, for he leaned forward, arms braced on his knees, his expression alive. "That's just it. He gave Job the same chance He gives us all. To know both His sovereign power and His loving character. Though God is powerful enough to speak the world into existence, He knows each of us in our very core. He knows our thoughts and our longings and wants us to seek His heart. King David said in the Psalms, 'Search me, O God, and know my heart, try me, and know my thoughts. And see if there be any wicked way in me, and lead me in the way everlasting.'"

Chogan had no idea who King David or the Psalms were, but the way Caleb's face lit with the excitement of what he shared ignited a longing in Chogan's own chest. Did Caleb really know this God so well? That was what Chogan had been seeking, a real knowing.

No matter how hard he tried to please the great spirit, to call on him for wisdom, he never seemed to connect. No response came, at least nothing that filled the longing inside him.

Footsteps pounded outside the lodge, breaking through their focus, and all turned toward the opening as the door flap was jerked aside. Telípe's youngest brother stood panting in the opening. "Meksem says those assigned to the morning guard should come quick. She said you and you and you are all part of it." The lad pointed to Caleb, Beaver Tail, and Chogan.

Chogan brushed the crumbs from his fingers and reached for his bow and quiver but kept his focus on the boy's next words.

"One of the guards saw tracks near the edge of the village. The cat must've come through after the rain last night, headed toward the woods. Uyítpe is angry it came so close and no one noticed him."

Beaver Tail nodded. "We're coming now."

Chogan stood with his weapons and started toward the opening as the boy sprinted off. Caleb and Beaver Tail would want a moment to say good-bye to their women, and he would rather wait outside.

He didn't dare poke his head inside Telípe's family's lodge, for she might be caring for the babes and need privacy. But if anyone came from that residence, he'd like to ask how her brother fared. The last word he'd had the night before was that Gezíu seemed to be resting well. No change yet in his fever, but that would need time to lessen as the poison left his body.

His disobedient feet took him in the direction of Telípe's lodge. He wouldn't go near the opening though.

The fussing of a babe sounded from inside, and his heart tugged that direction, making it even harder to resist. This lusty cry belonged to Éisnin. Kapskáps's voice had grown stronger since that first weak cry he'd heard from the edge of the woods the day of their birth, but her tone was sharper, not so full and lusty like her younger sister's.

The door flap waved and was jerked aside as Telípe stepped through the opening.

His heart leaped as it always did at the sight of her. Her face wore frustration, and she lifted the babe higher on her shoulder. Éisnin's cry grew louder as her mother bounced her.

Telípe met his gaze with a mixture of apology and that same exasperation the babe showed. "I'm sorry for the noise. I thought coming out in the sunlight would calm her."

The ruckus didn't bother him at all, but seeing the frustration on the faces normally so sweet and calm pressed him forward. When he reached Telípe, he held out his hands. "Let me take her." Not that he thought he could soothe the babe when her mother hadn't even been able, but he couldn't stand by without trying to help. No part of him would allow it.

Uncertainty furrowed her brow, but Telípe handed over the infant.

Éisnin's body was stiff as Chogan took her, cupping one hand under her head and the other supporting her rear. She was in the midst of a lusty cry when she must have felt the change in handlers, for the sounds stopped, her squinted eyes opened, and her mouth slackened. She studied him, her dark eyes widening as she took in his face.

He held her gaze, forming the same wide eyes and slack mouth she did.

"There." He kept his voice quiet and even, as soothing as he could manage with its deep rumble. "Your píke was right. You only needed something new to look at." At least she didn't seem frightened of him.

When the babe finally seemed tired of staring at him, her gaze swung to the sky above. He moved her to the crook of his elbow so she would be supported but still able to see around her.

At last, he shifted his focus to Telípe. Hopefully she wouldn't be offended that the babe had stopped crying in his arms and not her mother's. He was under no misconception that he had a touch more special than Telípe's with any little one. It was surely only the newness of his face that had distracted her.

But Telípe was watching him with something like amusement in her expression. A light lit her eyes that hadn't been there moments before. "Thank you." The corners of her mouth even tipped up in the makings of a grin.

But before he could coax the smile out in full, Beaver Tail and Caleb stepped from their lodge and moved along the path toward the place where the warriors gathered to be assigned their tasks.

Disappointment pressed in Chogan's chest. As much as he wanted to take down the wildcat before it brought harm to any more of these people, he wanted these moments with Telípe and the babe to stretch forever.

Maybe he could extend this one a little longer. He turned back to Telípe. "I have to go hear my guard assignment. Walk with me?" Accompanying him might make her a spectacle among her people. Others would begin to wonder if something was growing between them. Maybe they'd already begun to think that from their walk yesterday.

Would Telípe be concerned about her neighbors' opinions? Even if she weren't—after all, she'd not hesitated to stand up for him before—should *he* be concerned on her behalf? Would this put her at odds with her people or harm her reputation—being seen with a Blackfoot who wasn't quite trusted?

Even as he hesitated, she turned the direction Beaver Tail and Caleb had gone and stepped forward. She paused when he didn't come too, and she glanced back at him. Again, the corners of her mouth curved. "Shall I receive your orders for you?"

The impish glint in her eyes nearly brought a smile to his own mouth. Not only was she beautiful, but in moments like this, her playfulness lit the passion inside him. But the thought of bringing injury to her in any way—even to her reputation—squelched that flame. "Maybe it's better you're not seen with me. I'm Blackfoot. I don't want my presence to cause a rift between you and your people."

Her brows rose high. "You think I've ever worried about what others think of me?" She motioned around the camp. "They've known me since my youngest days. They've learned not to be surprised at anything I do." That twinkle slipped back in her gaze, and she waved him forward. "Come. I'm more concerned that you're not the last to arrive when called for duty."

A new surge of love climbed through him. She held the perfect mixture of wisdom and common sense, with enough playfulness worked in to warm his blood.

He stepped forward, and together they walked through the camp.

CHAPTER 16

*C*hogan stood at the edge of the gathering of warriors as the chief spoke his orders loud enough to be heard throughout this end of the village. Though Chogan was on the fringe, it didn't feel like he was on the outside, not with Telípe beside him and Éisnin perched in his arm, staring contentedly at the goings-on. Only the glare Pisákas sent his direction cooled the warmth inside him. The man stood on the opposite side of the gathered braves, almost as though putting distance between himself and Telípe. Or maybe that was only futile hope speaking. The last thing he wanted was to bring trouble to Telípe with others in her village, but he also couldn't stand the thought of stepping aside to let another man have her. Not without making his affections known and giving her the chance to decide.

"It must be killed." Uyítpe's vehemence bit through the morning air, breaking through his thoughts. "We let it come to the very edge of our village. That cannot happen again. I feel it here." He pressed a hand to his chest and gave a thump. "The cat will strike again soon. And which one of your children will be next?"

A tingle slid through Chogan with the words, and the babe in his arms grew heavier. What would he do if the wildcat attacked one of these helpless children? Or Telípe? Fear tried to surge, but he pushed it down, letting determination rise instead. Even anger. He would stop the beast if it took his last breath.

He refocused his attention on the leader as he assigned duties for the day. Caleb, Louis, Beaver Tail, and Pisákas were to guard the women who worked by the river. "They must continue harvesting the salmon, or we won't have sufficient stores for the winter. Even with the elk meat, we have many people to feed. Guard those by the river well." The man's gaze swept among the crowd, and it seemed to hover on Beaver Tail longer than normal. "Beaver Tail is in charge of that group." The Blackfoot brave had proved himself capable to these people, and he'd clearly become one of the most trusted.

That familiar longing rose up in Chogan's chest. If only he could be counted as such one day.

Then the man assigned braves to guard the four sides of the village, and both Adam and Hugh were numbered among the men chosen. Meksem had been hunting through the night, so she wouldn't be given a job today.

Since Beaver Tail was being sent to the river, Chogan likely wouldn't be assigned anything either. He didn't mind always accompanying Beaver Tail. He would learn everything he could from the man.

"Another group will hunt through the hills and trees toward the rising sun." He pointed through the wooded hills, in the direction where Chogan had gone the night of their first group hunt. "Follow his tracks but be stealthy. You must think like a wildcat."

He began to motion toward men as he called their names. "Tékes, Joel, French, and Chogan. I will go with you also."

Chogan stiffened. Had he heard right? The man selected one Nimiipuu brave, two white men, and Chogan—a Blackfoot not yet trusted? Perhaps he wanted a chance to watch him and the two white men in action and see for himself whether they could handle more difficult assignments. He would have the other man from his village with him to help, should one of them prove incapable.

Or worse, a threat.

Chogan glanced at Joel and French. Neither man was especially tall or broad, but from what he'd seen of them, they were more than capable. And they'd earned the respect of their group, which told Chogan everything he needed to know about them. Now he needed to make sure *he* didn't prove incompetent.

As Uyítpe dismissed the warriors, Telípe touched Chogan's arm. "I'll take Éisnin."

Though he hated to hand the babe over, he needed to hone his focus on the task ahead. But as he placed Éisnin in her mother's arms, he let his gaze linger on Telípe's face once more.

He wanted more than a simple good-bye. Urgency pressed through him. He needed to tell her at least a little of what burned in his heart. "Wait a moment for me."

She met his gaze, and though she seemed hesitant, she nodded.

With his heart hammering, Chogan joined the men who'd gathered around Uyítpe.

The chief scanned their small group, his gaze hovering on each man as he seemed to take that brave's measure.

Chogan did his best to show himself ready for anything that lay ahead.

Then the chief spoke. "Gather your weapons. Your sharpest knives, your straightest arrows. Your guns." He sent a marked look to Joel and French. Maybe that was one reason the white men were selected for this hunt. If only Chogan still had the musket his father had taken from him. "Bring food, for I know not how long the hunt will take us. We'll follow it until we stop this enemy of our village." The man's eyes narrowed with his words, determination lacing his voice.

"Bring extra water skins. I want nothing to slow us down." Uyítpe pointed to Chogan. "You, gather three of the flasks stored in the lodge where you were held. Telípe can show you which ones."

As the man gave orders for things the others were to gather, Chogan's mind raced ahead. *Telípe can show you which ones.* Finally, he would have a quick moment with her in relative privacy.

"We will meet at the cat's tracks near the edge of camp. Go."

Chogan spun at that last word and strode toward Telípe and the babe. She'd been standing back by one of the lodges but within range to hear the chief's orders.

He could feel the weight of her gaze on his face, but he didn't let himself meet her searching eyes. His blood was already burning hot enough. Instead, he touched her elbow and turned her toward the lodge where he'd been held those first days. She walked beside him without a word, and he had to force his stride slower to match hers. Probably most of the camp were focused on their own tasks, but there was no need to draw attention.

When they reached the storage lodge, he motioned for Telípe to enter ahead of him. She stepped in and moved toward a stack of flasks against the side wall. "These were made by the grandmothers—"

He couldn't wait a heartbeat longer. He knew about the flasks—he'd stared at them for days. Telípe was his only thought now. His body pulsed with her name, his mind heady with the sight of her, the scent of freshness that always hovered around her.

He reached for her arm, stepping near as she turned. Only the faint intake of her breath sounded before his mouth closed on hers.

Everything faded away except Telípe.

Nothing existed except this woman who consumed him. Her lips melded with his, giving and taking, stealing his breath in a dance as old as time. Had there ever been a moment when they weren't connected? Not just their mouths, as now, but their hearts. She'd woven so fully through him that, without her, he would shatter in a sea of fragments.

She pressed closer, and he drew her in, one hand around her waist and the other cupping her jaw.

Then something poked at his side, squirming. Sounds thudded against his awareness. Insistent.

He told himself to slow the kiss, yet his heart wouldn't obey.

The squirming grew firmer, and a babe's fussing finally broke through his senses.

Éisnin.

Reality seeped through him, and he pressed a final lingering kiss to Telípe's mouth before pulling back. He didn't quite have the strength to draw away completely.

He barely had the strength to stand.

Keeping a tight hold around Telípe's waist, he shifted to allow the babe room. That stopped her fussing, and he dropped his forehead to rest on Telípe's as their ragged breathing melded.

With his free hand, he slid his fingers over her cheek, caressing the side of her mouth with his thumb. So beautiful, every part of her. And softer than he would've imagined. How coarse was his own skin against hers?

He moved his hand down to her shoulder, sliding it along the length of her arm that held the babe. Then he wrapped his hand loosely around her back, enfolding mother and daughter in a circle.

He'd never felt anything so right as being with these two—like this. Though Kapskáps should be here too.

He'd shown Telípe his feelings, but he couldn't leave without speaking the words also. At least some of them.

"Telípe." His voice came out low and gravelly. He worked for more strength in his tone.

"Hmm." Telípe's voice held a dreamy quality, her eyes closed.

He wanted desperately to press kisses to those eyelids, but he'd better hold himself in check for now. Yet how did he say what he wanted? He'd never been a man of pretty words. All he could speak was the truth. "My heart...is yours."

She opened her lashes and pulled back enough to see his face. He didn't hide himself from her. Maybe it was too soon to reveal so much, but it seemed he'd felt this way forever.

She leaned up and pressed a kiss to his mouth, a touch so tender and sweet, he couldn't respond at first. When he finally found his senses to return the kiss, she'd already angled away.

With her hand, she cradled his cheek and stared into his eyes. "Return to me. We'll be waiting."

Only then did the sounds outside the lodge break through to him. Activity. Warriors preparing for battle.

She was right. He had to go. He had a mission to accomplish. But when he'd done everything he could to ensure her safety, he would return to her and the little ones.

He pressed a final kiss to her forehead, then leaned low and did the same to Éisnin's.

He straightened and met Telípe's gaze. "Kiss her elder sister for me too."

Telípe's eyes glazed as she nodded.

And with that final vision of them stored in his heart, he picked up the flasks and turned away.

*C*hogan bent low over the tracks to study them when it was his turn. These were definitely from the same cat he'd seen prints from before, not the smaller tracks he'd seen the day he discovered the black rock area. Those had been from the cat he'd killed, the one that had been warring with this larger animal over its territory. These were from the beast himself, prints that spanned almost double the size of Chogan's hand.

He straightened and stepped back in case any of the others wanted a closer look.

The chief had already started forward, searching out the next track. Chogan followed the same line as their group moved that direction. With the rain that had fallen early in the night softening the ground, it wasn't hard to locate prints often enough to know they were on the right path.

When the trail led them into the woods and up the first of the hills, the leaf-covered ground concealed many of the animal's tracks. Only when they found fresh wounds on a tree where the cat had sharpened its claws did Chogan breathe easily that they were still tracking correctly.

Onward they pushed, and staying on the animal's trail became harder with each hill they mounted. The chief possessed excellent ability to find signs that most would miss. The man had proved both a wise leader and capable. No wonder he'd obtained the place of honor in the village.

French, too, seemed to have excellent tracking skills, something Chogan wouldn't have expected from the quiet man. But as he watched him work, he wasn't sure why he should be surprised. French had told him once he'd been trapping for many seasons. He had likely developed good instincts about animals. Chogan should know more than anyone how little age sometimes played into abilities. Experience was what mattered, and if one started younger than most, that experience could be obtained earlier than usual.

As the cat's sign disappeared completely, the chief motioned for them to spread out, fanning through the area to cover a wider stretch of terrain. This was part of the same ground they'd searched the night of that first hunt, though Chogan was positioned a little to the north of that original stretch. He strained to keep his instincts alert, his senses keen.

Once, he caught a whiff of the pungent scent that came when a male staked its territory. He couldn't say for sure it was from the wildcat, but something inside him felt certain.

They stayed silent as they searched, with only the occasional sound of an owl's hoot to signal one of their group had found a likely sign.

The tweet of a songbird had been reserved for a significant sign that would require the others to come closer. Yet that bright sound never echoed through the trees.

They were climbing a steeper hill now, its surface rocky and almost straight up like a cliff, though it wasn't tall enough to be called a mountain.

Chogan had to use both hands and feet to scale the last stretch to the peak. He paused at the top to study the land on the opposite side. Scrubby trees dotted the stone surface near the top part of the downward slope, and thick tree growth covered the remainder of the way down.

No obvious sign of a wildcat appeared. No kill sites that he could spot from a distance. But then, he didn't really expect the animal to leave something so clear.

Yet that was one of the things that bothered him. They'd not spotted signs of the wildcat feeding. Surely a creature that large would need to eat at least every few days. During these summer moons, such a stealthy animal should be able to find enough food to grow fat. Perhaps hunger made the cat daring enough to come to the edge of the village. But the facts didn't settle right in his mind.

As he started down the stone-covered slope, he did his best to maneuver without grabbing trees that would rustle or loosening small stones under his feet that would make noises as they skittered downward.

Once, that exact sound of pebbles clattering echoed to his right. He jerked his gaze that direction and glimpsed the Nimiipuu brave sliding on his haunches over a steep part of the slope.

The man finally straightened, then proceeded more slowly. Chogan returned his focus to his own descent.

The surface of the rock he descended was changing from smooth boulders to broken, rough-edged stone. Places like this made him wonder how the mountains had been created. Had Caleb's God formed each nuance of rock and earth and trees and grass? So much creativity with so many different types. Could one Being really be responsible for it all?

He reached a place where the rock leveled off before dropping to a steep cliff. He straightened to ease forward and find the best way down the slope.

Cracking sounded beneath him, and a jolt shot through his body as the stone shifted.

The ground broke away under his feet.

A yelp burst from his mouth as he fell into blackness.

CHAPTER 17

elípe sat with Meksem and several of her friends in the lodge they all shared. The lodge Chogan stayed in too.

The men were out on their assigned duties, clearing the way for the women to accomplish the various things that needed to be done that day. Meksem had been sleeping most of the morning, recovering from her night of guard duty. But now she sat on her bed pallet sharpening her knife.

Kapskáps lay on the fur near Meksem, one tiny fist in her mouth and her eyes trained on her aunt. Though Meksem didn't speak much to the babe, every so often, her gaze would drift that way and linger on the child, soft pleasure glimmering in her eyes.

Elan had begun work on the evening meal, and Susanna and Colette were stitching moccasins, just as Telípe was doing. Éisnin sat propped in Telípe's lap, but she might need to be moved soon, for the babe's reaching kept getting in the way of her work.

"Your brother sleeps?" Susanna lifted her gaze from the leather in her hands to Telípe.

Telípe nodded. "He's done little else but sleep since this time yesterday, but his fever is almost gone. I think he's finally healing." She moved Éisnin's fist away from her stitching so she could see better. "Since Otskai took my younger brother to play with her son again, the grandmother finally sleeps now too. I think Ámtiz is grateful for the quiet." She sent a smile toward Meksem, one that her elder sister returned.

"She has been good for our family." Meksem's words might have been Telípe's own.

"She has been." Telípe reached to move Éisnin's fist again. The babe possessed so much curiosity. Too much sometimes.

"Let me take her, Telípe." Colette laid her work aside and reached out. "My eyes are too tired for any more stitching."

As she handed over the babe and the women's attention shifted to watch Colette play with the little one, a new warmth spread through Telípe. She'd never sat in the midst of a group of women as an equal like this. When she was a girl, sometimes she would join with her mother and the other matrons who came together to talk while they worked. But she'd always been a child, not part of the conversation. More of a nuisance than anything.

Yet these women counted her just like them, spoke to her as though interested in her life. They shared in the burden of her daughters. And in the sharing, the burdens turned to pleasure.

Even Meksem, with her warrior ways and the position she'd rightly earned among the braves, was accepted in this group. While the others stitched moccasins, she honed the blade of her hunting knife, yet she was an equal part of the whole.

Telípe glanced around at the group. Did she dare ask the question she'd been wondering more the longer she spent with these friends? Elan and Meksem had grown up in this camp, but the others—both women and men—had come from so many places. They'd met and joined together under hardships and trials, and maybe that was how such strong friendships were forged. But would they plant roots here? Or did they plan to go elsewhere after the two upcoming births?

She looked from Susanna to Colette. "Will you stay here, do you think? After your babes are born?"

The woman glanced from one to the other, Susanna looking to Elan and then Meksem. Meksem turning from Colette to Susanna, then back to Elan.

Finally, Elan turned to Telípe, maybe accepting her position as spokesperson for the four of them. "We haven't talked of what will come after the summer. This seemed a good place to rest and for the babes to be born." She sent a tender look from Susanna to Colette before turning back to Telípe. "We wanted to see you safely through your delivery. And meet these little ones." She leaned toward Éisnin and slipped her finger through the babe's fist. "They've stolen our hearts."

Then Elan straightened and looked back to Telípe with a shrug. "I think Otskai wants to see her cousin Watkeuse in the Nimíipuu village south of us. Before Watkeuse goes across the mountains again, I mean. Beyond that, we'll see where the Lord leads."

The last bit grabbed in Telípe's mind and she tipped her head to study Elan, hoping to uncover what she meant by the words. "You expect a sign from your God pointing to where He will send you next?"

Elan glanced at the others as a smile curved her mouth. "Maybe. It's not always that clear. God has a plan for each of us, and we've committed to place our lives in His hands. If He sends us a need to meet, we'll follow His leading."

Her words wove through Telípe's mind, settling in a way that felt almost familiar. She'd heard them speak before of the good path God had laid out for them. What struck her now, as it had in the past, was how they made God's leading sound so personal. As though they could speak with Him directly and hear a response.

As though their God truly cared, and not just for His desires to be carried out. But He knew them and cared for each of them. She couldn't quite put into words the difference, but it was there.

"You have questions, Telípe. I can see them in your eyes." Susanna's voice broke through her thoughts. Her smile was so open and encouraging...

The last of Telípe's defenses slipped away. "I want to know more of your God. Will you tell me of Him?"

Joy lit the eyes of each woman in the lodge. Susanna leaned forward. "You may have heard some of this already, but we'll start from the beginning, how God made the earth and loved the people in it so much that He was willing to give even the life of His precious child to save us." Susanna—and sometimes Elan and Meksem as translators—told the story of a love too deep to comprehend, and Telípe's spirit burned with its power.

Jesus, the Son of the great God who came to earth as a man, was a part she'd not heard before. She would have loved to meet Him, this man who people flocked to from as far as they could walk. But when Susanna spoke of His death, the sacrifice God made of the life of His son so that these people He created could be restored to Him—the burn of emotion clogged her throat, stinging her eyes.

Could she ever love anyone enough to let her sweet babes be killed? Not even for Chogan could she give up these innocent lives who depended on her. How could God do that? Why wouldn't He, if He was so powerful, find another way?

But as Susanna spoke of Jesus rising from the dead after He'd been in the grave three days, a tingle slipped through her.

He *had* found another way, a better way.

"Now we can know Him, Telípe. We can be His daughters and speak to Him as Father." Susanna's eyes shone with joy even as her voice trembled with emotion. "All we need to do is open our hearts to Him, let His spirit live within us, and commit to follow His good way."

She'd never heard the details laid out so clearly, and her heart longed to accept. To open herself to this God that Susanna described. Did she dare? It seemed as if she would be giving up control of her life to this Being. Could He be trusted?

She glanced around at the women again. They had all made this choice, given their lives to this God, and they seemed happier for it. Though they still endured the same things the rest of the people did, there seemed to be a light within those of this group. A strength that separated them from the rest.

She wanted what they had. Desperately, her heart had longed for something more. That longing had turned to hope during Susanna's story.

She met the woman's earnest gaze. "I want this too. Will you show me how?"

～

*P*ain seared through the blackness as Chogan lay on hard stone. Except it wasn't total darkness. A tiny bit of light filtered down from above, the hole he'd fallen through.

He'd landed on his hip and arm. It was the shoulder that throbbed as though a bullet had pierced it.

A shout sounded above, and he gathered himself, preparing to sit upright to see if any lasting damage had been done. His leg moved when he told it to, so maybe nothing in the hip had broken. The left arm was pinned beneath him, and by the way his hand didn't do as he commanded, he suspected something in the shoulder had been broken or knocked askew.

With his good arm, he worked his body onto his back. Pain shot through the shoulder, and he bit hard with his jaw to keep from crying out at the agony. His arm lay limp, angled out from his side.

"Chogan. Are you hurt?" The voice above spoke English, and Chogan blinked to clear his mind. Joel.

He forced his jaw to separate enough to grind out words. "Only my arm."

"I'm coming down."

Chogan squinted at the light above. The outline of heads appeared in the opening, but with the sun behind them and the pain pulsing through his body, he couldn't make out features. He must have fallen at least the length of two men. If they tried to come down, they would be injured too.

"Wait." Maybe he could find a way to get himself out.

"What? What is it?" Joel again. He must've heard enough determination in Chogan's voice to make him pause.

Chogan scanned what little he could see around him. The place seemed like a small cavern, maybe just a pocket in the mountainside the stone had closed off.

The hand of his good arm brushed something soft on the floor, and he picked it up. Fur. Like that of a...cat.

He moved his hand over the stone again, and more tufts of hair touched his fingers. An animal had definitely been here.

But how? There had been no break in the stone overhead before his feet created one. There must be another entrance, one that didn't come from above.

He grabbed the hand of his injured arm and cradled it across his belly, then strained to sit up. Agony shot through his shoulder, and he barely held back a groan.

But he was up now and could better inspect the walls around him.

There. A faint light in front of him.

"Chogan?" Joel's voice again.

Chogan lifted his chin so his words would carry upward.

"There might be an opening down the mountain, on the side of the cliff."

As rustling sounds and voices drifted from overhead, he called out, "Be careful. There might be other places not strong enough to hold you." He should have thought of that first. The pain was fogging his mind.

The light called to him. Hopefully the others would find the opening. Before Chogan moved, he needed to see what should be done with his arm. Laying the useless hand in his lap, he probed up the muscles, steeling himself against the pain.

No breaks in the bone that he could feel. When he reached the shoulder, a new leap of fire seared the joint. There seemed to be an extra bump behind the connecting point. He'd seen a shoulder joint out of place before. Had watched the agony it caused. But he wasn't sure how to get the bones back in place.

He tried pressing the bones, but the flash of light that ripped through his body nearly knocked him backwards.

He held himself motionless, squeezing his eyes shut as he willed his body to stay alert. He couldn't pass out, not with everything he had to do. Not with the others nearby.

At last, his body settled, leaving only the throbbing pain in the shoulder. Sounds of voices grew louder again, calling to him. He eased his eyes open and squinted toward the light. Had it grown brighter? The voices were coming from that direction.

Relief sagged through him. They must've found a way in.

"I see him." The English words held the lilt of a French accent.

Chogan finally saw the shift of a figure. French.

The man was wiggling on his side, which meant the opening must be barely large enough for him. Chogan's shoulders were broader than French's for sure. Even if he could manage to go out that way, the pain to his joint would be awful.

At last, French reached him. "Where are you hurt, my friend?"

Chogan motioned to his shoulder. "I don't think it's broken. Moved out of place maybe."

French scooted around him and dropped to his knees. "This might hurt." His hands started at Chogan's elbow, then with a few quick probes, worked up to the shoulder.

Chogan's entire body quivered as the agony rolled through him in waves. He did his best to stay motionless, but the pain couldn't be controlled.

French finally pulled his hands away, but it was several heartbeats before Chogan could relax enough to draw in a tiny breath.

"Hmm." He was studying Chogan, but Chogan didn't have the breath to ask what he found.

"The joint's out of place, all right. You have a big bump in the back where the bone moved. About the size of my fist." He held up a balled hand to help Chogan envision it. "I've helped put two shoulders back in place before, but I've never done it by myself. I think I know what to do though. Are you willing for me to try? If we can get it done, the pain will be a lot better right away."

Chogan worked on taking in a steady breath, then letting it out. Did he have a choice? The thought of the pain going away quickly provided encouragement enough. That was only *if* they could get the joint back in place. How much would he have to endure through that process?

"Do it."

"All right then." He scanned the length of Chogan, then looked around the chamber. "I'm going to need you to lie down."

Chogan didn't let himself think about what was coming, simply maneuvered as French told him to.

When he was lying on his back with his arm extended out, Joel's voice sounded from the side opening. "Everything all right in there?"

French turned that direction and called back, "His shoulder's dislocated. I'm going to set it, then see about getting him out."

Chogan couldn't make out the other man's response, so he simply focused on breathing again. In. Out. If it weren't for the throbbing in his shoulder, this would almost be relaxing. Maybe if he focused on that, the pain would ease.

French adjusted Chogan's arm again. "I'm going to move your hand up, and I want you to push against me as hard as you can. It's going to hurt, and hurt, and hurt. Then when the bone clicks into place, the pain will stop."

Chogan steeled his body. He could do this. He'd trained his entire life to do this.

French hadn't been lying.

Chogan bit down hard against the shooting pain, like a knife blade through his flesh. Burning. The fire heated more the higher the man lifted his arm.

A grunt slipped out. He clenched harder against other sounds. No more, he could take no more.

Then...a blessed release.

Chogan blinked to make sure he hadn't lost awareness. French still held his arm, but the shooting fire no longer seared his shoulder.

He gulped in deep drafts of air, letting the breaths clear his mind and fill his lungs. He'd made it. He'd endured.

"There you go." French began to ease his arm back down. "We'll keep this arm close to your side, and I need to find something to fasten it. We don't want this to move around for a few days, or the shoulder might pop back out."

Chogan let the man work as he focused on gathering his strength again. His body felt as weak as though he'd been through a full day's battle. French had found some kind of leather strap, maybe even cut from his buckskin tunic, and was wrapping it around Chogan's good shoulder and the injured arm.

Soon, Chogan would have to get up and attempt to slide through the opening. But before that, they needed to study this little cave better.

"French." Chogan's voice even sounded weak, so he cleared his throat to strengthen it.

"*Oui?*" The man pulled the knot tight, then leaned back and examined his work. "I think that should do it for now."

Chogan ran his hand over the stone floor and picked up a piece of hair. "I think this is wildcat fur. Do you think this might be his den?"

French's brow furrowed as he scanned the floor, then reached for something and held it up near his eyes. "You might be right. Sure does look like cat hair."

Chogan prepared himself for the pain of rising up, then launched into the effort. A twinge shot through his shoulder, but nothing more.

French held out a hand to help. "Take it easy."

He couldn't go easy, not until the wildcat was found, but he would do his best to safeguard the shoulder. Unless it interfered with finding the creature they hunted.

From a sitting position, he pointed to a place where the fur was pressed flat. "That spot must be where he laid."

On the opposite side of the small room, there was a small pile of something. A faint odor drifted to his nose, springing hope within him. Why hadn't he smelled that before? He pushed up to his feet and stepped toward the cluster.

Yes. Somewhat fresh, maybe even from early in the night.

French walked to his side and studied the pile. "You think he slept here during the rain?"

Chogan nodded. "I think so." Those droppings were definitely from the cat. And definitely less than a day old.

Chogan turned and scanned the area once more for anything he'd missed. Where would the animal go from here? After a good sleep, it had gone back to the village—or at least, it passed by the village. The tracks had been left after the rain. Was it searching for a meal? That seemed the most likely possibility. After a good sleep, the cat would be eager to fill its belly.

A frisson of fear swept through him. It would see the tempting meals in the village—all those innocent women and children. Would the cat dare stalk into the camp itself?

He didn't think so. The animal would likely lie in wait until an unsuspecting victim ventured away. It wouldn't be so foolish as to leave a place so full of potential food. That meant everyone in the camp was in danger.

No.

He spun toward the opening. "Let's go. I think we missed something along the way." Like...a set of tracks *toward* the village, where the animal had gone to fill its hungry belly.

CHAPTER 18

Telípe dipped her hands into the cool river water, relishing the sensation now that the heat of the day pressed hard. She lifted the liquid up to soothe her face, letting the drops trickle off her chin and down the front of her tunic. Too bad she couldn't reach Kapskáps in the cradleboard to let the babe feel the pleasure of the coolness. Both infants had grown so heavy, she'd begun carrying the elder in the cradleboard on her back and letting Éisnin play on the bank under a shade bush. The larger babe was simply too heavy to carry while she worked.

And she *did* have to work. This was the busiest part of their fishing season. If she didn't bring in food, there wouldn't be enough to last the winter. Even Ámtiz and their youngest brother were fishing—downriver with one of Ámtiz's friends.

Straightening, Telípe scanned the water's surface. She and the babes were working at one of the farthest points upriver, where the other women wouldn't scare away the fish. Beaver Tail hovered nearby, his gaze roaming every shrub and brush in search of the wildcat. They had so many guards watching during this fishing excursion, there was no way the cat could sneak close.

Seeing this particular Blackfoot brave always made her mind stray to Chogan. Indeed, not much could keep her thoughts from lingering on him. And that of course brought his kiss to memory, awakening every one of her senses.

She'd never connected with anyone as she had with Chogan in that moment. Or rather, *those moments*, for it felt as though there had been no start or finish, only a continual connection with him.

Even now, part of her traveled with him in the hunt, sprinting up hills, creeping through forests—wherever he was, he carried her heart.

An ache pressed through her. Was it simply missing his presence? Or was this pain part of their connection, where she now felt everything he experienced? Was he injured? Or had his illness returned?

If only she were there with him. Or better yet, him here and safe beside her.

An image of the four of them lounging at the river's edge slipped in, Chogan playing with the babes as though they were his own.

She pushed that thought away. She would never catch fish if she didn't focus.

While the sun streamed down, she managed to grab a few and place them in her pack. Not enough for an afternoon's work, but at least a start.

She would need to stop and nurse the babes soon, for they'd both begun to fidget and fuss.

She scanned the water's surface again, seeking out the darting shadows that signaled fish. Near the far bank, a few flashes signaled the movement she sought. She eased that direction, careful not to make a splash. On her back, Kapskáps squirmed. Unless the babe cried out, she shouldn't disturb the fish.

By the time Telípe reached the area where the fish darted, two shadows hovered in the water. She would have to be quick to get them both.

Positioning herself over them, she held her breath as she prepared. Then she plunged her hands into the water, grabbed an unsuspecting fish, flung it out of the river onto the far bank, and reached back under the surface for the other.

The second fish had startled, as she'd expected it to. She kept her gaze on it and reached for the place it would likely dart. Her fingers brushed the slippery surface of the animal, but she couldn't quite grasp it before the creature sped away.

The fish she *had* caught flopped on the bank, so she trudged to that side to capture it before it wiggled back into the water.

It would've been nice to catch both. Often, she was quick enough to grab two. But at least she had one to add to her pack.

On the bank behind her where she'd left Éisnin, the babe's complaints rose louder. She'd best take this fish back over and tend to her little ones. Especially now, when no one else was in sight. Maybe they'd have a few minutes of privacy. Beaver Tail must have gone downriver to check that stretch of his territory.

Slipping the fish into her pouch, she stepped back into the water and trudged through the current toward the bank where Éisnin's cries had now risen into wails. On her back, Kapskáps returned her sister's complaints, though the bouncing in the cradleboard seemed to soothe her a little.

A movement on the far bank caught Telípe's gaze. Farther back, away from the river about thirty strides, something flicked in the grass. She honed her focus on the spot, her senses jumping to alert, although she couldn't say exactly why. Now that she was looking, she could make out nothing out of the ordinary.

Then she saw it. Her heart stuttered, her chest pressed so no air would come in or out.

The wildcat.

The creature skulked low in the grass, almost the exact colors of its surrounding. But the beast was huge, longer than a horse from its nose to the tip of its tail.

And creeping their way.

Telípe charged through the water, pushing the liquid behind her with her hands to make headway against the waist-high current. Éisnin's cries must have summoned the cat, and its long slinking stride was closing the distance between them much faster than Telípe's scrambling through the water.

She tried to scream, but her throat closed off the sound. Her chest could get no air.

She couldn't let the cat reach her babe. With everything in her, she gulped in a breath, then loosed the loudest scream she could manage.

∼

"Check the outer edges of the village first. Look for tracks. Any sign." The chief spoke between breaths as they ran through the woods toward the camp.

Chogan's heartbeat hammered as he imagined what could be happening there now. Surely the wildcat wouldn't have attacked the camp itself. But what of those near the river? Would Telípe have gone to the water to catch fish? Surely she would have stayed with the babes in camp.

But Telípe wasn't the only one in danger. He didn't want *anyone* else hurt by the animal.

As they broke through the tree line into the stretch of grassland between the hills and the village, Chogan swept his gaze around the area. Nothing seemed amiss. A few figures moved among the lodges.

By the river north of the camp, he could see a form standing at the water's edge, and another walking downriver. Those long strides looked familiar. Beaver Tail? He was one of the guards assigned there, so probably so.

The chief pointed to the right side of the village. "Joel, French, and Tékes, circle that way. Chogan, come with me around the other side." The man shifted his stride toward the southern edge of the camp.

Chogan hesitated. Even as his feet followed the chief, his gaze wandered back to the river. Back to the place north of camp where he'd seen the figure standing by the water. The person was gone, though he could still see the guard walking downstream along the bank. There should be three other men guarding those by the river. Where were they?

A sound gripped his ears, and he strained to hear better. Was that a babe crying? He scanned the length of the river again. The sound might've come from the village, but something pulled his focus farther north.

"Chogan." The sharp bite of the chief's tone jerked him back to his surroundings. His feet had slowed to almost a halt as he searched. He needed to get moving, break into a run and catch up with Uyítpe. But the tug toward the river grew even stronger.

He motioned toward where he'd seen the person standing. "I think we need to check the water first."

The chief stopped and turned the direction Chogan pointed. He studied for a moment, then shook his head. "Beaver Tail is there. He would know if something wasn't right."

Normally, Chogan would've had the same confidence in the man. Beaver Tail had proved his intuition and abilities. But when Chogan's own instincts rose up so strongly as now, he couldn't go against them. He had to check the river.

A scream rent the air, cutting through him like a massive

claw. Chogan didn't wait to argue, just sprinted toward the source of the sound at the water's edge.

His heart pounded, and he heaved in deep breaths as he pushed his body faster, lengthening his stride. Honing his focus. Even as he ran, he strained to see any motion at the water's edge. Was he going the right direction? Across the open meadow, the sound could have reverberated. Maybe he'd not heard its source right.

He strained to push his body faster, to cover more ground, as he scanned the grassland. Scanned the river's edge. Strained to see across to the other side.

There. In the water, a head bobbed.

Was someone drowning? Maybe the river was deeper there than the other places he'd crossed. But no, the person moved upright in the water, the upper half fully visible. They seemed to be straining toward the bank, trying to reach something.

He pushed harder, willing his legs to strike as fast as the beat of his heart.

He searched the bank once more for what the person might be trying to reach. A movement clutched fear in his throat.

It was only a flash of motion, but the smooth cadence, the coat that nearly blended with the grass...

The wildcat.

At least thirty long strides separated Chogan from the bank where the cat was aimed. A new sound broke through his focus. A wailing cry.

A babe.

Fear scrambled his thoughts, cutting off his breath so he could barely draw wind to run.

Not Telípe's daughters.

His gaze moved back to the person in the river, but before he laid eyes on her, he knew.

Telípe.

She wore the cradleboard on her back but clutched no baby in her arms. That missing child must be lying on the bank.

The cat was slinking toward the crying baby. At least it wasn't sprinting in a full out attack.

Chogan reached for an arrow from his quiver with one hand and his bow with the other. But his left arm wouldn't move where he told it.

A new bout of panic welled as he jerked against the strap French had used to tether the injured limb to his side. He writhed to free the arm so he could draw the bow, but the tie held fast.

He had no time to fight with it. He'd already lost too much time trying to retrieve the bow. The cat was slowing too, sneaking up on the babe as though curious. The child's cries hadn't scared the animal away, only drawn it nearer.

Throwing the bow and arrow to the side, Chogan pushed back into a hard run, drawing his hatchet this time. If he could get close enough to aim the blade at the beast's heart, he could stop the attack. Then with his knife, he could finish off the animal.

Ten strides away now. He aimed and flung the tomahawk in the quick motion he'd practiced hundreds of times, taking into account how quickly the animal was moving so the blade would strike just behind the front shoulder.

The animal seemed to hear the blade coming, for it leapt forward the moment he released the handle. The cat landed on the ground in a crouch, ducking the tomahawk as it sailed over the top of his back. The wooden handle struck the cat's topline, and it hissed, flicking its tail in an angry snap.

A massive paw swung down, landing hard on the ground.

Not the ground.

A scream ripped from Telípe just as a baby's wail filled the air.

Chogan surged forward to close the final strides between

him and the cat, drawing his knife and raising it high to plunge. If only he had both hands free to wield the knife, but the strap locked his injured arm tight against him.

The cat saw him coming and straightened to all fours, it's back arching, readying for battle. The wailing didn't cease, and Chogan risked a glance at the ground beneath the animal. The beast had one mighty paw planted on top of the baby's belly. Staking its claim.

Anger pulsed through Chogan. *Not yours. Mine.* With everything in him, he lunged the final step, driving his blade downward with his good arm, slamming his entire body into the thrust.

The knife struck the cat, and a mighty hiss filled his ears, morphing into a furious howl as the beast spun, jerking itself away from the blade.

Chogan landed hard on the ground, his knife penetrating the earth. Pain shot through his sore shoulder, but he ignored it. Clutching the handle, he scrambled to his feet and jerked the blade out of the ground, then raised it high again.

Some wildcats might have run, but this one crouched to fight.

Fury surged through Chogan's veins as he coiled to engage in battle. This war he would win. He had to draw the cat away from the baby.

The beast sprang at him, its jaw cracking open to reveal fangs as long as Chogan's fingers.

Fear gripped his chest, but he clutched tighter to his knife blade and prepared for the strike.

As the animal lunged, Chogan ducked and swung right, twisting to plunge the knife in what he hoped would be the beast's chest.

Its tough hide caught the blade, holding the metal suspended for a heartbeat before the tip poked through. Yet that tiny delay kept the knife from pushing far into the animal.

The cat's momentum drove it forward, away from Chogan's blade. The animal rolled, then came up with a powerful lunge. It had moved away from the babe, but not far enough. Telípe wouldn't be safe to run in and scoop up the child.

Chogan barely had time to gather himself as the next attack came. From the edge of his awareness, a voice sounded. Telípe?

The beast was upon him, striking a powerful blow with its front paws on his chest. Chogan braced himself with the knife, and the point of the blade slammed the animal's head.

A fierce cry emanated from the cat, almost a squeal, as the blade must've struck something painful.

The animal whirled backward, rolling off of him. Chogan scrambled to his feet, readjusting his grip on the knife handle with his good hand. He probably hadn't inflicted a deep enough wound to stop the creature, but maybe it would be distracted enough to give him a moment for strategy.

But the animal only shook its head, clearing its senses for the next attack. It crouched for another spring.

This time, Chogan stepped backward, drawing it farther away from the babe. At the corner of his vision, Telípe stood ready to dive forward and get the child at her first chance.

He had to give her that chance. This fight was between him and the cat only.

As he took his second step backward, away from the infant, the cat coiled to spring. Chogan braced himself, preparing the knife. He would let the beast use its own momentum to drive the blade into its chest. All he had to do was stand firm. If only he had *two* good arms to hold the knife steady.

As the wildcat leapt into the air, its jaw opened again, its teeth flashing in the sunlight. Nearly blinding him with a stab of fear.

An arrow flashed at the corner of his gaze, striking the cat. The animal only twitched with the hit, but the blow was enough to lessen its force as it plowed into Chogan. He stepped to the left, just enough to miss the powerful jaws and land his knife in the broad chest.

Once again, the thickness of the hide made it hard for the knife to penetrate. The force of the animal pushed back against Chogan as he used everything in him to hold the blade steady.

At last, the point plunged through the skin and into the flesh beneath.

The creature convulsed. It tried to draw back, but Chogan kept his grip on his knife handle through sheer desperation.

The animal twisted beneath him, and Chogan bent low to hold the handle. He couldn't lose his only remaining weapon. The beast shook its powerful head, slamming the massive skull against Chogan's own.

A flash of light blinded him, then blackness surged in. As hard as he tried to keep his hold on the knife, the handle pulled away from him.

No. He fought to push the blackness back, but it hovered, closing in.

Voices sounded around him. The cry of a babe.

Then, nothing.

CHAPTER 19

*T*elípe surged forward and scooped up Éisnin the moment the cat and Chogan rolled far enough away from the babe.

Clutching her daughter close, she darted away—far away. Tears streamed down her cheeks as her heart twisted inside her.

Save, Chogan, God. Don't let it kill him. Please.

Even as a peace settled over her, fear tried to overwhelm. She had to keep her babes safe, yet how could she stand by and let Chogan be mutilated by the savage beast?

She turned back to check on the pair. Maybe his blow had finally maimed the animal. In truth, how could any creature still fight with so many wounds? She'd seen Chogan strike it three times with the knife.

Yet as she watched the animal, the massive size of the wildcat swept through her again. He was huge. The power in those paws and the bone crushing teeth. How could any man win against it?

Then another movement beyond the pair caught her notice.

Pisákas. Running toward them. Bow drawn, arrow arcing toward the wildcat.

Oh, God! Had he come in time? *Please. Let him save Chogan.* Surely he wouldn't let his anger toward the Chogan stop him from killing the wildcat.

Pisákas was only ten strides away now and sprinting hard. She looked back at the cat and Chogan. The animal was still moving, pulling away from Chogan's body. But so much slower this time.

It backed far enough away for her to see the man on the ground, and a new cry broke from her chest. Chogan lay still. Motionless.

No, God! He couldn't be dead. *Get up, Chogan. Please, Lord.*

Pisákas reached the beast with his tomahawk raised and slammed the blade into the cat.

Another guttural roar surged from the animal. Then it slumped to the ground, its feet buckling beneath it. The creature lifted its head once more, and this time its roar came weaker, with a bit of a mewling cry in the final notes.

Pisákas raised his tomahawk once more and planted the blade in the wildcat's side.

Its head dropped to the ground, as still as the man lying beside it.

Pisákas straightened and looked her way, his gaze scanning to see if she or the babes were injured. Éisnin whimpered in her arms, but there was no sign of blood.

Telípe pointed to Chogan, her heart aching. Too much emotion clogged her throat to speak.

As Pisákas turned to the man on the ground, his expression shifted. Not to anger or triumph...but to sadness.

Grief washed through Telípe as she started toward Chogan. She couldn't bring herself to pass by the cat, so she traveled wide to approach Chogan from the other side.

Others were coming now. Beaver Tail and the chief and a few warriors running their direction. Where had they been when Chogan needed help?

She should have done something more than stand helpless from a distance. But what could she have done with Kapskáps on her back? Her focus had been to get her children to safety.

Chogan had fought the cat with the last of his strength. Paid for their safety with his life.

She dropped to her knees by his blood-smeared face. He lay with his head turned to the side. Where was the blood coming from?

She brushed a strand of his black hair away from his temple, letting her thumb caress the skin there. She'd never touched him so freely, but she let herself now. If only she hadn't waited until this moment.

If only she'd told him how she was coming to feel. She never had, though. Even after their kiss. He'd said his heart was hers. But she'd not said how much he'd won her own heart. Only that he should return to her.

I meant alive, *my love.*

His skin twitched, and she stilled. Had that been only his body's final reactions as it faded away? Even as she told herself to believe the worst, hope soared within her.

"Chogan." Her voice broke on his name.

Beside her finger, his eyelashes shifted. Parted.

His eyes opened. Only halfway, but joy burst inside her. She moved her hand to stroke his hair again, working her fingers between the strands. "Are you alive?"

His eyes roamed over her, but his gaze didn't seem focused. Then his lids drifted shut again, but his lips parted. He seemed to be struggling for sound.

Oh, Lord. Thank you!

His mouth worked, and a word finally came out. "Telípe."

Tears surged again as her joy bubbled out in a laugh. She bent low over him, as low as she could with the babe still in her arms. Though a crowd was gathering around them, she gave them no notice.

Instead, she leaned near his ear. "I'm here, my love."

She needed to find out where he was hurt. Needed to get him back to the lodge where he could be cared for.

But he spoke again. "The babe?" His eyelids cracked open. His gaze shifted around, searching.

Telípe maneuvered Éisnin where he could see her. "She's here. Not hurt, I don't think. Thanks to you. And to God."

Chogan's eyes drifted closed once more, and the corners of his mouth curved in a smile. "Only God."

Joy swept through her and she lifted her face to send a prayer of thanksgiving heavenward. Her gaze caught on Pisákas, standing a little apart from the crowd.

He watched her and Chogan, had surely seen the love that connected her to this man—this Blackfoot brave. Would he try to make more trouble, even after Chogan had nearly given his life to kill the wildcat that endangered their people?

But it wasn't vengeance in Pisákas's expression. As his look softened, the corners of his mouth eased, and his head dipped in a nod. His gaze dropped to Chogan, and the glimmer in his eyes showed acceptance more clearly than any words could have spoken.

～

*I*n the lodge a little while later, Telípe dropped to her knees by Chogan's side, her heart aching as she studied the gash and swelling on his head. He lay propped on rolled furs, but as she settled beside him, he struggled to sit all the way up.

She touched his arm. "Stay where you are."

He didn't cease his efforts, though a frown of pain wrinkled his brow.

"Stubborn man. Lie back or I'll leave."

Chogan stilled, though he'd worked himself upright by now.

His gaze met hers, and he must have seen the determination in her expression. He eased back down to the bedding with a smile at the corners of his mouth. "Stay."

She slid her hand down his arm, and he twisted his palm so her fingers landed in his, a fluid dance, as though they'd practiced the act many times before.

His brows rose. "The babes are well? Not hurt?" Again that crease formed across his forehead, this time a line of worry.

Telípe gave him a reassuring smile. "Not hurt at all. Both have full bellies and are snuggled on their sleeping mat." She glanced at his cut face again, then moved her gaze downward to where his tunic covered the wound on his chest. "I'm sorry I wasn't here to help you." Her daughters had been so hungry by the time they all returned to the lodges, she'd had to make them her focus at first.

"My wounds aren't bad. Elan cleaned and salved them." His thumb stroked the back of her hand.

She inhaled a breath, her mind going back to the terror of the attack. Her fear for Éisnin. The helplessness of pushing frantically through the water, unable to reach her daughter as the giant cat skulked closer and closer.

Then her desperate hope when Chogan appeared, running faster than she'd ever seen a man—as though a giant hand lifted him above the earth and carried him to reach the cat just in time to stop its attack on her sweet babe.

Then the new rush of fear when the animal landed atop Chogan. His first strike didn't kill the beast. Didn't even slow it down.

Then the second attack. The cat rolled away with barely a pause before it spun and lunged again for the man. Her terror had been split for her daughter, still dangerously close to the battling pair, and for Chogan, the focus of the wildcat's rage.

He fought with only a knife, and as far as she could tell, with only one hand. How could he possibly overcome such a giant beast with so little in his favor?

In that moment, her heart had cried out to God for his safety. For the first time in her life, she'd had a Greater Power to turn to in her darkest time.

And as she'd cried out, a peace like a giant pair of sweeping wings had wrapped around her.

She'd reached the shore, and as soon as Chogan drew the wildcat far enough away, she grabbed up Éisnin. Though terror had continued to claw at her throat, that peace had been like a barrier.

"You're thinking of the wildcat?" Chogan's words rumbled low, drawing her back to the present.

The concern in his gaze sent a fresh surge of love through her. "I suppose we'll all be thinking of it for a while."

There was something he'd said afterward that tugged at her the more she thought about it. Maybe now was the time to ask. "When I was trying to cross the river to get to Éisnin before the cat reached her, I prayed. Not to the great spirit, but to God. The God that Meksem and Susanna and Elan and the others have taught me about."

She needed to tell him that story, but that could come later. "Though I prayed, I still feared. But when you were battling, I cried out with everything in me for God to save you. I felt this strong peace, like wings wrapping around me to calm me the way a mother bird calms her little ones. Then, after Pisákas came and ended the cat's life, you lay without moving. I thought you were gone. I thought the peace had been wrong."

Emotion stung her eyes, and she fought to keep them clear. "But He did save you. I should have trusted the peace. I should have trusted the God I have now promised to serve." Now for her question. "When you awoke, you said to give thanks to God. Did you mean the great spirit?"

Chogan shook his head but paused in the act as his eyes

narrowed in a grimace of pain. After a moment, he said, "I've been listening to Caleb read from the book that tells the words of his God. I think He's the God I've been searching for. I want to know more of Him. I want to know this God who not only made the world and all people but knows them still—and answers them when they call to Him. Caleb says He has a good plan for every person."

A tingle swept through Telípe as Chogan's words filled her up, bubbling joy inside her. Not only would he not resist this God, but his longing matched hers. Together they could learn more about Him. Together they could come to know Him and be known.

A sound behind her turned Telípe's attention to the lodge opening as Susanna stepped in. After ducking through the entrance, she straightened slowly, one hand supporting her large belly and another braced at her back. Something about the expression on the woman's face sent a ripple of alarm through Telípe.

She turned more fully to face her. "Susanna, are you well?"

Susanna sent her a look that may have been an effort to smile but was more grimace than anything. "I'm sorry to disturb you. I'm just going to lie down for a while."

Telípe studied her as she waddled across the room to the bed pallet the woman shared with Beaver Tail. She could tell the moment Susanna's pain loosened, easing away. Was it too early to be her time? Telípe counted the days in her mind. Maybe a little earlier than Susanna had said, but not much.

Telípe needed to call Elan and someone else to help with the birth. And Chogan would have to leave this lodge. She glanced at him, but he was already studying her.

When their eyes met, his gaze held a knowing. "Where should I go?"

"My brother's lodge. I'll ready a bed for you there. But let me get help for Susanna first."

He gave her hand a squeeze, and the touch made her want to stay at his side. But a soft grunt from Susanna's direction replaced that longing with an urgency.

Releasing Chogan's hand, she stood and moved toward Susanna. The woman might have already realized her time had come, but just in case, Telípe would speak to her first.

But she'd only crossed half the distance before a whooshing sound whispered through the air. Then the gurgle of liquid.

If Susanna hadn't realized before, there could be no disguising her time now.

~

Telípe had never seen anything as intimate or soul-stirring as the moment Beaver Tail rested his gaze on his wife and newborn son.

Susanna lay propped on a clean fur, deep shadows under her eyes from the challenges of the birth, the babe nestled on her chest. Telípe stepped away from Susanna as the man approached.

Wonder emanated from his expression, and he padded forward as though the space around mother and child were hallowed. Joy seemed to roll off him in waves, but he never made a sound.

Susanna watched him, her face glowing, even with exhaustion dragging her features. Her mouth curved in the most beautiful smile as the strong brave she called husband dropped to his knees by her side.

He took her hand, and as his other hand reached up to stroke the hair from her face, their eyes locked in a conversation too intimate for anyone else to watch.

Telípe backed away, moving to stand with Elan by the lodge entrance. Her throat swelled with emotion—with the wonder of the babe's birth, of new life, and the beauty of husband and wife as Beaver Tail leaned close to his son and cradled the dark hair with his large hand.

With the pleasure came a pain that ached in her chest. She'd not had a moment like this. Heinmot had never been able to meet his children.

Did she dare open to the possibility of another chance for this joy? Her love for Chogan burned deep within her. She'd meant to tell him, but Susanna's labor pains had come before she had the chance.

She *would* tell him though. She would tell him everything in her heart.

Let him be part of Your good path for me, Lord God. But no matter what, help me follow where You lead.

CHAPTER 20

*T*his moment was better than any other in Chogan's life.

He sat with Kapskáps propped against the curve of his leg as he played with her tiny fingers. Nestled against his side, Telípe held Éisnin in a similar position. The two babes had such different personalities and reactions, and watching their expressions brought a smile deep inside him.

With a gentle breeze blowing across the river and the three people he loved best here with him, this place where he'd fought a wildcat only six sleeps ago now seemed like paradise.

In truth, anywhere he could be with these three would be paradise.

"Look how she grabs your finger and tries to sit up." The laughter in Telípe's voice brought the smile up to his face.

Kapskáps did seem to be trying to sit upright, though she could barely lift her head off his leg.

"She's a fighter, this one." He slid a glance at Telípe with a grin. "We'll have to watch her. In a few years, she may be hunting wildcats like her Aunt Meksem."

Telípe pursed her mouth in a disapproving look. "No more wildcats."

He slipped a hand behind her back and pulled her closer, pressing a kiss to her soft hair. "No more wildcats. Or any other danger, if I can help it. Not for the three of you."

For a moment, they sat like that, but Telípe was thinking something. He could feel it in the thickness of the silence between them.

When the babe released his finger, he moved it to Telípe's chin and pulled back enough to raise her face so he could see her eyes.

Her gaze was troubled, and a weight pressed in his chest. If it were in his power, he'd never let anything worry her. He'd give her reason only to smile.

She searched his face. "Chogan, what now?"

What now? Was she asking about his intentions toward her? Surely she didn't question his feelings. Yet he'd never put his plan into words.

Not that he really had a *plan*. Only that he would go wherever she wanted, or stay here if that's what she chose. She probably *would* want to live here. With such a village around her, with this much acceptance, how could she ever wish to leave this place? Did he dare hope they would let *him* stay?

He *did* hope. But maybe he was getting ahead of himself. Telípe needed an answer. Then they could work out the rest.

As much as he didn't want to move away from this position with her pressed against his side, what he had to say was important. And he wanted to see every thought that floated across her face. Any concern that might darken her eyes.

He shifted, turning his body so he could see her fully, adjusting the babe so she was still comfortable. Now he could see all three of them clearly.

He locked Telípe's gaze with his own, and once again, her beauty quickened the beat of his heart. "I want to be yours, and you mine." He motioned from Éisnin to Kapskáps. "I want to be their father and raise them knowing they're loved, not only by you and me, but by the God Who created them." The liquid warmth in Telípe's eyes caught his breath. "I want to be your husband. To protect you and keep you with food and everything that pleases you. And if our God wills it, I want to give our daughters more sisters and brothers to play with."

Telípe's eyes rounded, her gaze darkening even more as a shy smile played at the corners of her lips.

Those lips.

Maybe he should wait for her to answer, but her mouth and the look in her eyes drew him. An answer without words.

He closed the distance between them and brushed his mouth against hers.

Pure sweetness. The taste of her, the sweet power of her kiss, was a gift he would never tire of, as long as he lived.

EPILOGUE

Telípe had never seen a white man's wedding ceremony. Meksem had already been married to Adam by the time Telípe returned to this village heavy with child. So she'd not known what to expect for this joining of Colette with the man whose eyes shone with love anytime she came near.

In some ways the ceremony, with them standing before each other and Caleb speaking words from the Bible—God's words— was more formal than she'd expected. The Nimiipuu considered a wedding to be more like a meal—a feast.

But the words were beautiful. Spoken in English first, then translated into Nimiiputimpt. Emotion clogged her throat as she listened.

Two becoming one flesh, as planned by God. She'd never considered that marriage itself was created by Him. That He blessed and made a union holy if the man and woman entered into it the way He willed.

She glanced at the man beside her, the one whose arm slipped around her, holding her close.

They'd not yet said when they would wed. Soon, that was all she knew.

But now, an urgency pressed through her to make sure their union was God's will. That He would bless and make their marriage holy.

Chogan caught her gaze, and the warmth in his eyes said he felt much of what she did. She would have to share all her thoughts when they had time alone.

She refocused her attention on Colette and French as Caleb—the minister, they called him—motioned to the pair. "What God has joined together, let no man separate." Then his warm smile spread as he shifted his focus to French. "You may kiss your bride."

Heat flushed up Telípe's neck at the intimacy between the pair. A kiss like that wasn't often paraded in front of an entire group.

But as French and Colette turned to face them all, the radiance in Colette's smile nearly stole Telípe's breath. She was always beautiful, but this joy that emanated from her made her shine like a glittering star.

Telípe could imagine what that happiness felt like. She tasted it every time Chogan looked at her. But the joy that spilled out of Colette now raised the sting of tears to Telípe's eyes. Happy tears. Tears full of hope for what would come to them. Soon. Blessed by God.

Something at the edge of Telípe's vision caught her focus. Chogan had turned that way, too, watching two riders approach the village from the south.

They rode spotted horses, and the person in the rear seemed smaller, maybe a child.

Others were noticing the visitors, and a low murmur spread through the group.

Otskai must have recognized the pair, for she moved toward them, working her way through the crowd. She walked a few steps onto the stretch of grassland as she raised her hand to shield her eyes from the sun.

The riders were near enough now to see clearly they were a woman and child. The girl couldn't be more than seven summers old. They reined in when they reached Otskai, and the woman leaped to the ground and wrapped Otskai in a tight hug.

A sense of expectation filled the group as Otskai returned the embrace, then helped the child down and walked with the pair toward the wedding party.

Telípe had never seen these strangers, so she glanced at Meksem to see if she knew who they were.

The expression on Meksem's face was hard to read. Not her usual warrior mask. Maybe curiosity? She must have felt Telípe looking, for she turned and leaned close to murmur, "It's Watkuese, Otskai's cousin who we brought back from the Shoshone camp. The girl is her adopted daughter, Pop-pank."

Telípe nodded understanding. She'd heard the story, and Otskai had mentioned wanting to visit her cousin again before Watkuese returned through the mountains to the Shoshone camp.

Was that why the woman had come now? To spend time with Otskai before setting off on that journey? But if this was Otskai's cousin, she must be Nimiipuu also. Why would she wish to leave her people again? Maybe she'd married a Shoshone brave.

Telípe leaned near Meksem. "She has a Shoshone husband she's returning too?"

Again, that odd expression crossed her sister's face. "No. Not a husband."

Who then? Telípe turned her focus back to the woman, who was moving freely among those gathered for the wedding. When she reached Susanna and Beaver Tail, who stood only a few steps away from Telípe, Susanna embraced the woman freely, as though they'd long been friends. Then Watkuese bent over Susanna's son, and her face transformed. Her manner stilled as she studied the child, wonder marking her features.

When she looked up at Susanna, a longing touched her gaze. A yearning that seemed to place a sheen over her eyes. Did she too long for a child of her own? She had Pop-pank, but maybe she wished for more.

Telípe leaned into Chogan's arm around her. She could well relate to that longing for more. And God was fulfilling her every desire, one by one. First with these two babes. Then with His own spirit that she couldn't seem to get enough of.

And now with this man, whose love showed itself in new and wonderful ways every day. The blessings surrounding her exceeded everything she'd ever imagined.

Did you enjoy Chogan and Telípe's story? I hope so!
Would you take a quick minute to leave a review where you purchased the book?
It doesn't have to be long. Just a sentence or two telling what you liked about the story!

To receive a free book and get updates when new Misty M. Beller books release, go to https://mistymbeller.com/freebook

ABOUT THE AUTHOR

Misty M. Beller is a *USA Today* bestselling author of romantic mountain stories, set on the 1800s frontier and woven with the truth of God's love.

She was raised on a farm in South Carolina, so her Southern roots run deep. Growing up, her family was close, and they continue to keep that priority today. Her husband and children now add another dimension to her life, keeping her both grounded and crazy.

God has placed a desire in Misty's heart to combine her love for Christian fiction and the simpler ranch life, writing historical novels that display God's abundant love through the twists and turns in the lives of her characters.

Connect with Misty at <u>www.MistyMBeller.com</u>

ALSO BY MISTY M. BELLER

Call of the Rockies

Freedom in the Mountain Wind

Hope in the Mountain River

Light in the Mountain Sky

Courage in the Mountain Wilderness

Faith in the Mountain Valley

Honor in the Mountain Refuge

Brides of Laurent

A Warrior's Heart

Hearts of Montana

Hope's Highest Mountain

Love's Mountain Quest

Faith's Mountain Home

Texas Rancher Trilogy

The Rancher Takes a Cook

The Ranger Takes a Bride

The Rancher Takes a Cowgirl

Wyoming Mountain Tales

A Pony Express Romance

A Rocky Mountain Romance

A Sweetwater River Romance

A Mountain Christmas Romance

The Mountain Series

CPSIA information can be obtained
at www.ICGtesting.com
Printed in the USA
LVHW091618191021
700868LV00001B/11